Tequila Mockingbird

Tequila Mockingbird

LEWIS C. HASKELL

Another 'Finn Pilar' Key West Mystery

ABSOLUTELY AMAZING eBOOKS

Published by Whiz Bang LLC, 926 Truman Avenue, Key West, Florida 33040, USA

Tequila Mockingbird copyright © 2016 by Lewis C. Haskell. Electronic compilation / print edition copyright © 2016 by Whiz Bang LLC. Cover design by Judy Bullard.

For information contact:
Publisher@AbsolutelyAmazingEbooks.com

ISBN-13: 978-1945772016 (Absolutely Amaizng Ebooks)
ISBN-10: 1945772018

To Susan,

"Grow old along with me! The best is yet to be, the last of life, for which the first was made.

Tequila Mockingbird

Chapter One

THEY WERE DOING Tequila shots. It was the third round that killed him; not the tequila shot, but the thirty-eight caliber one as they played Russian roulette while screwing their brains out, in this case quite literally. I listened to Stacy describe her client and the first thought that went through my head was natural selection wins again.

I know that's probably harsh but I could just picture the scene. "Hey, babe, watch this," as he spun the chamber and had her put the gun to his head. He took a bite of lime, a lick of salt from the top of her breast then tossed back the tequila and told her to pull the trigger as he came. At least they were playing with a revolver not an automatic. Now that would have been really stupid, although with these two, degrees of stupid is a distinction without much of a difference.

Stacy's call had interrupted my morning exercise routine. I was sitting in the bar at the Southernmost Café sipping a Bloody Mary and preparing for my daily swim. Crutch and I had already been on our early morning bike ride around the island. In the case of Crutch, my three-legged dog it truly is a *ride* in the basket.

I have been recovering after my last case and now have only a couple of scars to show for being stabbed, shot and hooked by a fishing gaff trying to survive my crazy ex-wife and her gay lover. I know it sounds weird and it was. Stacy my lawyer then, lover now, and I had a wonderful two months together after the case was over and before she moved up to Tampa to work at a law firm there.

It seems that this client she was calling about was a Key

West local who had gone to high school with Stacy and wanted her to handle the case. Stacy was a local girl made good which could not be said of her client.

As it happened, I knew her client Trixie, a *performer* at a local adult entertainment emporium known as *Pussy Galore*. You are safe in assuming it is not a ballroom dance studio and she was not a contestant on *Dancing with the Stars*. Before you think ill of me, I was not a client of her establishment. She had helped me on a previous case sharing the name of an ex-boyfriend in the drug world. It sounded like her choices in men hadn't improved.

Trixie was apparently doing a bit of crystal meth with her latest beau, the now deceased Rocco Ramon. Rocco was a three-time loser who she said claimed to be an entrepreneur. I suppose having a small meth lab up on Sugar Loaf Key counts. They were in her trailer on Stock Island just one bridge north of Key West when he pulled out his *gun*.

He also carried a .38. It seems Russian roulette during sex adds to the rush. They began doing tequila shooters and ultimately .38 shots. I can't imagine meth, tequila and gunpowder are a good combination but it seemed that Rocco had been ingesting too much of the former and ultimately the latter. *At least he went out with a bang in more ways than one.*

Trixie was brought in for questioning when they found gunpowder residue on her hand. I guess the authorities consider Russian roulette when someone else pulls the trigger to be murder. She began to sober up and she used her call to reach out to Stacy, hence the call to me.

"Finn, Trixie is not the sharpest knife in the drawer but she is not a killer. Can you pick her up when they release her and put her up at your place till I get down tomorrow? Talk to her and see if you can find out anything that might help with this case." she asked.

"Seems pretty open and shut, babe. What are you thinking?"

"It seems that Rocco told her he had loaded the gun with a blank so she couldn't be hurt however, the cops are saying that she owed Rocco money for the meth she was using. He was taking it out in trade and she had finally had enough so she substituted the blank with a live round. Big difference between premeditated murder and death from misadventure."

"Ok Stacy, anything for you . . . . for my usual fee, of course." I could hear her snicker and she promised, "Trust me, I miss you too. I will be down tomorrow and we can . . *debrief.* "

"I look forward to a wild night of debriefing," I smiled and returned to my Bloody Mary. After a moment's reflection, I put in a call to my former partner on the Key West Police force leaving a message asking him to call me.

~ ~ ~

The deep blue waters of the Atlantic beckoned so I left Crutch in the tender care of Cindy the bartender at the Southernmost Café and took off on phase three of my daily routine, a swim to one of the channel markers and back. It takes about thirty minutes and at this time of year the water is warm and the seaweed minimal. By the time I returned, Cindy had phase four ready for me. *You can't drink all day unless you start in the morning.*

Actually, my first Bloody Mary of the morning is a virgin but I have an image to maintain as one of Key West's resident degenerates, so I keep that on the down low.

OJ had called back during my swim so I returned his call. "What do you need?" he growled.

"I just wanted to hear your happy voice on this beautiful day," I said disingenuously.

"Bullshit, Finn, you only call when you need something and it is always a fine day on the Rock."

"OJ, that's why you are a detective; your breathtaking insights," I said as I smiled.

"Fuck off, Finn." And he hung up. People are always hanging up on me.

I waited a few minutes and called him back. "What?" he snarled. I guess my number came up on his smart-ass phone.

"Before you hang up again, can you tell me anything about the idiot who shot himself up on Stock yesterday?"

"What do you think I am Finn, your personal CI"?

He loves to use cop speak like CI for confidential informant, perp for perpetrator and vic for victim.

"Come on OJ, it's a simple question. The story in the paper today just gave his name and the location. I figured you might have some details."

"Finn, what are you, a PI now? You're going to have to get your info from someone else on this one dude. It's a murder investigation and I didn't catch it."

"Since when did Russian roulette become murder?" I asked. "Rumor had it this was just natural selection in Bubba world." Bubba is the local Key West name for longtime residents of the Rock.

"Finn, I don't know where you get your info but this is at best manslaughter and at worst, first degree homicide. Besides, what's your interest in this case?"

OJ is a friend so I lied. "Guy's name was familiar so just curious."

"Yeah, right," he said and signed off.

~ ~ ~

OJ and I had worked together for almost eight years having joined the force around the same time. I was new to Key West arriving with my then wife Courtney who was both beautiful and connected to one of the oldest families in Key West.

I rang out of BUD/s, the Navy SEAL training program

due to a back injury during training, technically a Drop on Request or DOR. After six months of physical therapy I signed up for EOD or Explosive Ordinance Disposal. I managed to avoid blowing myself up during two tours in Afghanistan but eventually realized that I didn't know too many *old* EOD guys. I left the Navy after four years.

I met Courtney in a club in San Diego one drunken night and she seemed impressed at the time with my tales of derring-do. She wasn't a *frog hog* hanging around McP's on Coronado but she was easily impressed. Our whirlwind courtship lasted through her final exams at USD studying real estate and we got married at some Elvis-themed chapel in Vegas.

In hindsight, I think it was all just intended to piss off her father, who after hearing of the wedding, threatened to cut off her inheritance if she didn't return to Key West. I was bored with the accounting job I had picked up again after leaving the Navy. I was doing audits for a bunch of San Diego defense contractors so I jumped at the chance to go live on an island. I had trained in Fleming Key for my Spec Ops dive certification and loved the climate and island living.

Courtney's father, Roger Linebush an influential Bubba, twisted some political arms and got me a job on the Key West Police Force. KWPD seemed thrilled to have a bomb disposal expert on the force. In me, they saw an opportunity for new toys like robots and maybe even an armored personnel carrier for the SWAT team. Little did they know what the future held for the Linebush clan and me.

Police work while married to one of Key West's royalty usually meant pretty soft assignments. I would always get the call to be the local liaison (read muscle) whenever Jimmy Buffett or Kenny Chesney came to town.

I was once cruising down Whitehead very early one

morning as the sun was rising over the Southernmost Point. I noticed an attractive blond in tight-fitting stretch Lululemon joggers and a red-hooded Ohio State sweatshirt running down the street being chased by a heavily muscled black guy.

Now Whitehead runs through an area in Key West known as Bahama Village. Today, a transitioning neighborhood, it was for many years the home of the black families in Key West. All the usual stereotypes ran through my head; damsel in distress, being chased by the big bad wolf - she even had the red hood. I made a quick U-turn, raced ahead of her, and turned about a block in front blocking a one-way street next to the Old Stone Church on the corner of Whitehead and Julia. I called for backup, flipped on the bubble lights and jumped from the car.

The damsel came jogging up as I jumped from the car. I drew my gun, pointed it over her shoulder at the man chasing her and yelled, "Stop, get on your knees and put your hands behind your head."

She skidded to a stop and dropped.

In hindsight I guess she thought I was pointing the gun at her. The big bad wolf stopped, slowly raised his hands and in a calm voice said, "Good morning officer."

Needless to say it gave me pause.

Slowly the woman looked up and said, "Officer, before you shoot Bernard, perhaps I should introduce my protection detail and myself."

I stood, gun pointed at Bernard as Lady Gaga slowly removed her hood and I suddenly felt very awkward.

While never a huge fan, she is one of the more recognizable stars in the world. Here I was with her on her knees in front of me pointing my gun at her. Well, you get the picture.

Slowly I lowered my weapon. I also holstered my gun.

After a few moments, while I helped her up and

apologized to her and Bernard, we had a good laugh. After that interesting introduction whenever she came to town she would ask for me to be her *protection* for her morning jogs and Bernard got the morning shift off.

While celebrity liaison work was fun and life in paradise not a hardship, I eventually started to get bored. Even for a twelve year old kid, Baskin Robbins can get tedious once you have been through the 31 flavors a couple of times.

I was looking for some real police work. Maybe it was the adrenalin I had lived on in Afghanistan doing bomb disposal. I just needed more action. I requested a reassignment to the Drug Task Force that worked closely with the DEA and Coast Guard to find and prosecute the coke and marijuana smugglers and even more importantly now, the meth labs.

Much to my dismay given my accounting background, the powers that be in the bureaucracy decided I was better suited to focus on financial crimes and assigned me to the fraud squad. Not exactly the most exciting role and I began to wonder who I had pissed off.

It may surprise you, as it did me, but financial fraud is actually an issue in tourist towns like Key West. With over two million visitors a year and being the number two wedding destination in the country, we see a lot of scams: everything from bachelor and bachelorette parties at Gentlemen's Clubs that over bill on credit cards (how dumb or drunk do you have to be?), to the sale of overpriced retail cosmetics. Not exactly bomb disposal in Afghanistan but better than protection detail for the rich and fabulous.

My first case seemed like a small potatoes tourist fraud involving a three thousand dollar bag of face creams. I know, you are wondering how desperate I was for something to do. At first when I interviewed the *victim*, I could see why she would pay just about anything that promised to upgrade her looks. It was clear that she had already tried just about everything possible by way of surgical enhancements and was now looking for a miracle cream.

Even so, I guess she concluded that three grand for a few two-ounce jars of Manatee sperm stem cells was a *bridge too far* for eternal youth. I suspected one too many margaritas at Sloppy Joe's might have been involved so her caveat emptor instincts had been suppressed.

This was not the first time this particular emporium had been drawn to our attention but it seemed that when caught they simply admitted to a small mistake of an extra zero on the charge slip that took the bill from three hundred to three thousand dollars. Oops, my bad and here is your money back.

Now to me, even thirty dollars is more than I would even consider spending on face creams but I am told it is not unusual for some people. Being the inquisitive type, I decided to subpoena the store records for the last year and discovered after several days of digging that this *little oops* happened about twice a week usually for between five hundred and twenty-five hundred dollars. Given that our last complaint was almost six months ago, I estimated that they were overbilling by about three thousand dollars a week, or more than a hundred and fifty thousand a year. Now we were talking major fraud.

After quietly returning the originals, I thanked the owner. In the spirit of just being thorough I asked for and received the corporate documents. I determined that ownership was complex with dividends being paid to a series of corporations in the Caymans. To my surprise I recognized one I had seen before.

It was listed on some documents my wife had brought home to review as part of her management of her father's businesses. In addition, the corporations owned six other store locations around the island. If this same *little oops* was going on in all the other stores, it could amount to over one million dollars a year. *This could get awkward.*

In addition to the retail operations, I began to review the property tax roles and found the same ownership group owned the real estate in several of the buildings where the retail stores were located. A further review of the rents paid by the cosmetics store revealed long term leases with rents in significant excess of market rates. These guys were double dipping and probably flipping the properties based on the rental rates and long leases.

As it happened, before I had a chance to complete my investigation, a very unpleasant family dinner interrupted my efforts. But I digress . . .

Chapter Two

GIVEN MY HISTORY with Trixie who was an informant in a previous case I worked on, I felt it was only fair to help her out. I packed up Crutch on my scooter and we headed over to the Green Parrot. The Parrot on Whitehead is one of my favorite watering holes and Trixie had introduced me to one of the locals known for propping up the bar most days and for the occasional drug related interaction.

As I walked in, Billy saw me enter and seemed to shrink down on his stool. I expect he would have skipped if he didn't have a half a pint of some dark beer sitting in front of him.

Crutch and I slid onto the bar stools on either side of him. Crutch prefers the stools to the floor. I ordered a Bud light for him and a Stella for me.

Before you get all PETA (People for the Ethical Treatment of Animals) on me, I am not being cheap; he just prefers a light beer at this time of day.

"What are you drinking, Billy?" I asked in my usual friendly voice.

"IPA," he sneered.

"Well, aren't you the craft beer aficionado?" to which he paused, looked puzzled and replied, "I ain't no afisha . . . whatever."

"Aficionado, doofus. It's like a connoisseur." I paused, but it was still not registering. "Never mind," I replied shaking my head.

I called the bartender over and ordered another IPA for him.

"How's tricks? I inquired.

"What do you want Finn? You ain't no cop so I don't

gotta talk to you."

"I am just making a little friendly conversation with my old friend Billy," I replied smiling back at him. "Just catching up on local news."

"Yea right," he mumbled and finished off the first IPA then started on the one I'd bought him.

I think he was afraid I'd take it back and he wanted to make sure he pulled on it first. I'm surprised he didn't backwash it. *Maybe he did.*

"Billy my friend, I wanted to see if you have been in touch with our mutual friend, Trixie? I asked.

"In touch, right I get it" he snickered.

"Not *that kind* of in touch doofus. Get your mind out of the gutter," I replied before I realized I was probably asking too much.

"Have you seen her? I paused, "and not in the biblical sense" which was followed by another blank stare from him. Too obscure I thought. "What's she up to?"

"What's it to you?" he asked taking a long slug of beer to finish it off.

I waved to DJ the bartender for a refill. "I heard she had a new boyfriend, that's all," I said priming the pump.

He smiled, "What day is it? She always has a new friend, usually every hour," then chuckled at his own wit.

"I heard some guy named, Rocky or Ricco or something like that," I said.

"You mean Rocco," Billy slurred, "He's a real dick."

"So you know him?"

"Yeah, he owes me money."

This was a real surprise as Billy was usually the one who owed others money. "What could he owe you money for?" I asked.

He smiled and pointed at his again empty glass. Damn this guy can put away beer.

I took ten bucks from my meager roll and put it on the

table holding it under my fingers. "What for?"

"He was trying to meet an old friend of mine for some special inventory. He offered me fifty bucks for the intro and another fifty if it worked out. He owes me the second fifty."

Boy, this guy is really brain dead but then again I am the guy who just bought him two beers.

"Now give me the ten!" he demanded.

"A name, Billy? " I growled.

"I want my fifty," he grinned.

Hmmmm, maybe not so dumb. I pulled another ten spot from my stash and put it next to the first.

"All or nothing asshole."

He paused, looked at the twenty bucks and caved like I knew he would. "What the hell?" he slurred. "It's a guy who goes by Squeaky, a mechanic over in Garrison Bight."

You could have knocked me over with a feather. Squeaky and I had a history and suddenly this case just got a whole lot more serious.

"What was he looking to buy?" I asked trying not to sound too rattled.

"That is going to cost you, Finn," he smirked.

"Screw you Billy," I swore as I slipped off my stool and walked out of the bar leaving Billy yelling after me to cover the tab. I flipped him the bird and pointed out the twenty I left on the bar to DJ. *I'm not a complete idiot.*

* * * *

Crutch trailed behind as I walked across Whitehead to my scooter and we headed to Schooner Wharf, one of the two hangouts where you could usually find Squeaky.

Squeaky had a history including an arrest I made about four years ago when I caught him in a sting selling used engine parts from boats moored out on the back side of Wisteria Island off Key West. He was advertising parts on Craigslist for boats he knew were moored long term, then when he had a buyer he would go out at night and steal what he needed.

He served two years for it then went to work for my ex father-in-law for a while then was fired by him. On my last case, he tried to run me over with his truck but that is another story.

Schooner Wharf is another of my favorite run down, dirt floor, cold beer bars located near Jimmy Buffet's Key West studio on the main harbor. Schooner's is surrounded by a restored schooner, a high-end craft brewery/restaurant and a trendy new hotel - sort of a turd in the punch bowl at a Four Seasons wedding.

It gives me a chance to pick up cigars from my favorite roller Miguel who has a small stand inside the bar. I sat at the bar and chatted with Suzie the bartender. She brought over my usual Bud Light and I fired up a Robusto. I figured at some point Squeaky would show up.

Crutch was doing his usual cute one-legged dog tricks routine including his newest, a salute with his one front paw touching his eyebrow. It took me about a month during my rehab to teach it but a bit of tape above his eye as he tried to brush it off was enough for him to learn how to do it.

I rescued Crutch a couple of years ago and we have become a fixture around town. He has developed quite a routine as we go from bar to bar.

My phone rang and I saw it was Stacy. I love these new smart-ass phones. "Pilar Escort Service," I intoned. "If you're down for it, we're up for it!"

She chuckled, "I take it you're on your smart ass phone Finn."

"It's a nice ass phone when you call," I quipped.

"Enough already. I will be in Key West in a couple of days. I just called to let you know they are releasing Trixie today. Seems they don't really have enough to charge her," then she paused. "Can you put her up at your place for a couple of days until I get there?"

"I appreciate your confidence in my selfless character. Of course, I will. When does she get released?"

"They said at two o'clock today, so if you can meet her at the lock up on Roosevelt and take her back with you, that would be great. I'll put her up at my place when I get there. It's just for a couple of days."

"No problemo. I'll finish lunch then drive over there."

Stacy hung up and I called Suzie over to order lunch and another Bud. Crutch had finished off my first one after his show.

I usually order the Pirate cut burger that is a ten once prime rib burger topped with braised ribs and a bacon poblano sauce but I have to watch my weight so I asked Suzie to box half. OK, so I can resist anything except temptation.

As it arrived, Crutch took on such a pitiful look that I had to cut a chunk for him. As I was about to take my first bite, in came Squeaky.

He took a look around the bar, saw me and took off.

"Shit," I said out loud.

"Suzie, please box both halves and I'll be back to pay and collect it. Keep an eye on Crutch and don't feed him anymore," I yelled as I took off after Squeaky.

He had a head start but obviously had been drinking all morning so his run was more of a stumble. Of course I can't be critical because I had started my day early as well. By the time I caught him we were up by Dante's on the dock and headed to West Marine.

I grabbed him by the collar and dragged him into the parking garage near the ferry terminal for a little privacy.

"So Squeaky . . . . " I began.

"Fuck you Finn. I ain't done nuf-fink wrong," he mumbled

"Squeaky, Squeaky, Squeaky," I said in my most

patronizing voice. "Just walking into Schooner's is a violation of your parole." I paused for effect. "You know, use or possession of alcohol is a no no, so I could get you back inside in a heartbeat if I wasn't such a nice guy," I smirked and sat him down.

"Now I ran into an old friend of yours at the Parrot this morning and he told me you owe him fifty bucks."

"I don't know what Billy told you but he's a liar," Squeaky replied.

"I didn't say it was Billy."

Squeaky paused as I watched the wheels grinding. It was a painfully slow process.

Finally he said, "You're trying to trick me, Finn. I don't owe Billy nuf-fink, if he made a deal with the guy then that guy owes him not me."

"Who did you tell Rocco to see, Squeaky?" I asked.

"I dint tell him to see nobody," he slurred. "I duh know where to get that stuff."

"That was a double negative dumb ass. If you didn't tell nobody then you must have told somebody, so who?"

"Jesus Finn, where do you come up with this stuff?"

I thought back to Miss Mathews in sixth grade pounding it into me.

"So what was Rocco looking for?" I asked.

"You're going to have to ask Rocco. I ain't no snitch," he retorted.

Clearly news regarding Rocco's untimely demise had not made it into Squeaky's network yet.

"Look Squeaky, I am only concerned for your well-being." OK I don't really give a shit what happened to him. He had tried to kill me by running me down several months ago but I needed information.

"Here's the deal dude." I paused. "Rocco was shot in the head last night and I am afraid you could be next. If I can find you, so can the person who killed him. So what was

Rocco looking for?"

Alright I was not being fully candid with him but I was within the ballpark.

Squeaky leaned over and threw up on my sandals and his own sneakers. Damn, and on my feet as well. I liked these sandals.

"Shit Squeaky. I can try to protect you but I need to know what Rocco was looking for."

He started to shake and stuttered, "Dddamn I nnneed a ddrink."

Given the money I saved by not paying Billy, I pulled out a ten and said, "What Squeaky?" waiving the bill at him.

He burped in my face. You will need to imagine how delightful that was and blurted, "Something called bulk sicho effrin I think."

"What?" I marveled at his intellect.

"I don rightly recall but it sounded like that. Sudo or sicho something."

I paused, "Pseudoephedrine? I asked.

'That's it," he said seeming pleased with himself.

Small things and small minds. Damn, just what we need, a new source of drugs in Key West.

Ephedrine is a crystalline alkaloid drug that causes constriction of the blood vessels and widening of the bronchial passages and is used to relieve asthma and hay fever. It is also a main ingredient in methamphetamine or meth or crystal.

It made sense that Rocco who was a small time meth dealer would want it but what happened to his current supplier? It seemed like a reasonable question to ask. Was he going around his current guy? Was he looking to expand and that was not appreciated?

"Squeaky, why was he looking for it? He's already a meth dealer."

"How the fuck should I know?" he said looking like he

might throw up again.

"All right, did he say who wanted it?" He burped again and I jumped back to avoid more of his *gifts*. He took off stumbling.

I could have caught up to him but I figured there was no point as he probably didn't know.

What the hell was Rocco up to and why?

* * * *

I headed back to Schooner's to pick up my burger and collect Crutch. I walked in to find Crutch snoring heavily under a stool with a way too contented look on his face. I picked up the go box with my burger and it felt way too light. I nudged him with my foot; he stirred, opened one eye and burped.

"Damn, Suzie, how much did you feed him?"

She looked over sheepishly and said, "Jeez, Finn he was doing his show for the other customers and things got out of hand. His back flip was a showstopper and he had three encores. We saved you some fries."

"Thanks, for nothing," I bitched then offered, "Never mind, just order me a salad with salmon to go." I sighed heavily.

With the salmon salad in a box and Crutch stumbling along trailing me slowly, we walked to the scooter and he hopped, literally, onto the floorboard. I was amazed he could even walk after nine ounces of prime rib and short rib burger. We took off to pick up Trixie at the local lock up on North Roosevelt.

As we drove up Eaton toward White Street then across to Truman, I reflected on how much my life had changed in the last six months.

Thanks to my ex Navy SEAL instructor Matt Divine, I was a licensed private insurance investigator and the off again-on again boy toy to a beautiful, young Tampa-based attorney.

From a peaceful, slightly impoverished, slightly buzzed Key West lifestyle to a newly minted bar owner about to launch Key West's first hopefully trendy Tequila bar.

Life was good but little did I know about the road ahead.

Chapter Three

I PULLED IN to the parking lot just as OJ was walking out of the building. I told Crutch to stay and strolled over to meet my old partner. Crutch trailed behind me.

OJ observed my instructions to Crutch and quipped, "Well trained dog you have Finn. What's your secret?"

I turned and noticed Crutch behind me. "Stay means follow me and piss on the first person I talk to," I said to him. "That be you," I chuckled.

OJ watched Crutch with caution for a second then said, "No dogs in the station, Finn. You know the rules."

"He is my 'emotional support dog,'" I laughed. "You aren't going to deprive a wounded veteran his service dog are you?"

OJ shook his head and continued walking to his car.

As I walked into the station I said to Crutch, "Now I'm going to have to get you one of those cute little vests with Service Dog on each side but if you keep eating those burgers like today, it will need to be an XXL in no time." He ignored me and we walked up to the desk to see if Trixie was ready to go.

I remembered Sylvia the girl behind the desk from my days on the force and couldn't resist having a little fun.

"Sylvia, you are looking unbelievable. Have you been working out?" putting on my biggest most smarmy smile. I felt like that character on the old fifties TV show *Leave it to Beaver* who was always sucking up to June Cleaver. Can't remember his name.

Now you need to understand that Sylvia is a thirty-year veteran of the department having been on the front desk for most of that time. She has been getting donuts from a parade of ambulance chasing lawyers looking for referrals, defendants' families looking for inside information and cops looking for office gossip to brighten their boring day.

"Oh Finn honey, you are such a sweet talker. I know you like those skinny little bitches but I would bet you've never been ridden by a full figured girl, have you?" she said as she smiled sweetly.

If you met Sylvia, full figured would not do her justice. I would bet she tops out at four hundred and fifty pounds, but I have seen her in town shaking it with a cross section of guys every weekend for years. She has been married four times and has outlived them all. Some less generous than I have called her *The Black Widow* but I have always enjoyed our repartee.

In a moment of irony, I offered her my salmon but with a sly wink she simply said, "Fuck you Finn, you know I don't eat that shit."

To which I replied, "Of course, but I forgot to get your favorites and it is all I have to give."

"Maybe next time," she smiled. "How can I help you?"

"You have a guest." I paused. "A person of interest, who is to be released today at two and I was asked by her lawyer to pick her up."

"You running an escort service these days, Finn? I heard you were Key West's newest drinking establishment entre . . . pre . . . neur."

It is true that I am a partner in a new bar but more on that later.

"It's a favor for a friend Sylvia, nothing more."

To which she replied, "You don't need to get all defensive now Finn. Would that friend be that skinny bitch, fancy pants, tiny butt Tampa lawyer I heard you were *involved with*?"

I was at first a bit nonplussed, but then I remembered a homily my dad used to say. 'Telephone, telegraph tell a woman or tell the hefty girl behind the desk at a police station . . . .' I can't remember it exactly but it was something like that.

"Well yes, as a matter of fact she is," I agreed. "Stacy is her name and she called me and asked me to pick up her client."

"Are you a client of our *guest* as well?" Sylvia queried while raising a carefully styled and penciled eyebrow.

"Please Sylvia, you have no need to be jealous on that account, honey bun. I am but a humble chauffeur."

Sylvia heaved herself up from her probably grateful oversized desk chair and over her shoulder called out, "OK sweet cheeks, let me go fetch her before we steam up the room any more than it already is." She then disappeared through a door to the jail.

Crutch and I cooled all five of our heels in the Spartan waiting room scanning two-month old copies of House Beautiful and Coastal Living.

Who was the magazine buyer for this place? Probably the Chief's niece raising money from subscription sales for her cheerleading squad's trip to the quarterfinals in Jacksonville. They hadn't heard of Field and Stream or Rod and Gun?

All right, so I did quietly tear out a recipe for coconut shrimp with a mango chutney dip from a Coastal Living. No one here was going to use it.

~ ~ ~

Trixie came out of the back with one of the guards and Sylvia in tow. Trixie was dressed in a ragged one-piece shift that looked a bit worse for wear and her hair was three day greasy. If it was possible she was thinner than when I had last seen her several months ago and her eyes were hollow with dark shadows smudged above her sunken cheeks. It looked like her intimate relationship with meth was further along than I had anticipated.

She looked a bit confused and when she saw me a flicker of a smile crossed her face then disappeared. Sylvia gave her a manila envelope presumably containing her personal items. She signed for it then turned to me.

"I know I have seen you before but I don't remember your name. Was it at the club?" She smiled again revealing a missing tooth among mostly yellow ones.

This girl had gone downhill fast since I met her just a few months ago during my last case.

"Trixie, my name is Finn and I'm a friend of Stacy your lawyer." I paused to let that sink in. "She asked me to pick you up and take you to my place for a day or two until she gets down here from Tampa."

She hesitated then said, "I ain't got no money to pay you," adding an attempt at a seductive smirk. Again with the double negative. I let it slide.

"Stacy is a friend of mine so you don't need money," I told her. "Why don't we get you back to my place and cleaned up?" I offered.

She asked, "Can we stop at the club first so I can pick up some clothes and my last pay check?"

I had never thought about how strip clubs paid their girls but the club known euphemistically as a *gentleman's club*, is Pussy Galore and not far out of our way. I agreed. Actually, nothing is very far out of your way in Key West.

As the three of us loaded onto the scooter I flashed to how much those of us in Key West can haul on our scooters. I have carried bookshelves from Home Depot and table lamps from Pier One without a second thought. With Crutch on the floorboards, Trixie on the back and my salmon salad in the milk carton carrier, we headed to Pussy Galore.

As we road over the Palm Avenue bridge toward Eaton Street I turned and said to Trixie, "Once we get you settled I have a few questions about Rocco and what happened."

At first she hesitated then said, "They told me we were making a video for something called YouTube so I went along with it to make a few extra bucks."

I almost drove off the road. *They? Who were they?*

"Trixie, who are *they* and what kind of video?" I inquired.

"Rocco and his friend said it was an adult video."

Not helpful. "I sort of get the point of the video but who was his friend?"

As we pulled into the empty parking lot she said, "Let me get my stuff and we can talk back at your place."

It was two thirty on a weekday afternoon so the place looked pretty deserted. I asked her, "Is it open and can you get in?"

"Oh sure," she said. "It's after the lunch crowd and before happy hour so the girls generally go home for a couple of hours of sleep but the bartender is there to cover the door." She bounced through the front door with more energy than I had seen since I picked her up.

I turned off the scooter and sat on it in the shade waiting for her. Midday sun in Key West on an asphalt parking lot is the epitome of a tropical oven.

From my days in the war zones of Afghanistan, the muffled explosion was muted but unmistakable to my trained ears. I leaped from the scooter and raced for the door. As I reached for the handle, the door burst open and a big scruffy hulk in a pair of cut offs and a t-shirt reading, 'It's not pussy but it's finger licking good' staggered out coughing. Colonel Sanders must be rolling in his grave. Who writes this stuff I thought as I scrambled into the building.

Smoke was coming from a door in the back so I rushed passed the stage and the bar hoping to find Trixie perhaps injured but alive.

It was not to be.

As I stood to one side of the door, all my EOD training came back in a flash. I was not expecting a secondary device here intended for the first responders after the primary killed the original target, like we often faced in Afghanistan, but old habits die hard. As I stepped inside the door to the rear of the building, I noted the row of lockers located along one wall with several knocked down and buckled.

As I stepped into the room, I was greeted with an all too familiar site from my EOD days. Blood and body parts slammed against the wall opposite the lockers and covering the dressing tables, mirrors and ceiling.

The first time I saw this, I like most, puked and cried, knowing I had lost a friend. It became an all too familiar sight during my tour.

Fire was beginning to consume the room so I tried to see what, if anything, I might discover before it was burned beyond recognition.

Today brought back those terrible memories but mentally I shut down knowing there was nothing I could do to help whoever was vaporized by the explosion. Rather than disturb the scene that the fire was rapidly consuming, I stepped back into the bar and listened for the sirens that would foretell the arrival of emergency services.

This was not something our local EMTs, Fire and Police would be prepared to face. If nothing else, I might be able to help as they began to comb the ruins of the dressing room of the club.

I thought back to Trixie's comments regarding the other person in the room with she and Rocco and the video they were shooting. Once it was confirmed that she was in fact the deceased, then unless she was a random victim, it was at least a theory that someone wanted to shut her up.

The door to the bar slammed open and two firefighters rushed in, their hoses quickly dragging through the building to the rear. They paused when they saw me and one came over to see if I was OK. I assured them I was and he continued to the back door. His partner came out of the room and had clearly thrown up into his breathing apparatus at the sight of the room now almost engulfed in flames.

His partner rushed in to see what was inside and began to douse the flames. Smoke had begun to billow out of the room and into the bar so I made my way out of the club leaving the fire fighters to do their job. I needed to call Stacy.

Outside in the oppressive afternoon heat of the parking lot a crowd had gathered and I saw my old partner OJ interviewing the bartender. I waved and decided it was time to go before he wanted to talk to me. Once I got home I ducked into the house and called Stacy.

"Well of all the phones in all the world, you had to call mine," she said seductively as she picked up. "Sup big guy? Were you able to get Trixie all tucked in safe and sound?"

I paused not sure what to say. "Stacy, there has been a problem," I began.

"What kind of problem? The department said she would be released at two o'clock so if they gave you a hard time, I am going to ream then all a new one." Her voice went up about an octave.

"Stacy, I picked her up fine and I ran her over to the club to pick up some fresh clothes and her paycheck."

"And?" she asked.

"Stacy, when I dropped her off she went into the club and a few minutes later there was an explosion."

Her voice shifted immediately to concern. "Was she hurt? Is she all right? What happened?"

"Stacy, at this point I can't be sure but between the explosion and the fire, it does not look good for Trixie. If she was in the room where it happened, then . . . " I paused. "She may not have survived."

27

"What do you mean, she may not have survived? You were right there! Can't you tell?" she screamed.

"Stacy, the fire department is still fighting the fire and until we can get into the room we can't identify any . . . . " Again I paused, "Any evidence."

This was a new thing for Stacy and I was doing my best to avoid saying, we would need to use DNA from what we could scrape off the walls to identify her.

"Stacy, she may have gone out the back door of the dressing room before this happened and until we can confirm things, we can't make any assumptions."

"I asked you to make sure she was safe Finn. How did this happen?"

Shit now this is my fault? "Stacy, I am doing everything I can to figure this out and I will keep you in the loop with any progress."

"Right, like you kept her safe," she snorted. "I am on my way and should be there in about four hours. I want some *progress* when I get there." And she hung up.

~ ~ ~

I put in a call to OJ and then headed over to the bar. Before you think ill of me for going to a bar, I had promised my new business partner that I would stop by to see how the leaseholds were progressing. We were days from our grand opening and I was in charge of making sure we were ready for a flawless launch.

Now for the uninitiated, Key West has over three hundred bars and restaurants so a logical question would be *why build another one?* After all, the population is only twenty-five thousand full time residents. But we have over two million visitors a year with many coming for weeks or months at a time.

It is not hard to miss the crowds wandering the streets at all hours of the day and night including bachelorettes sporting pink tee shirts saying 'Emily's Last Night as a

VIRGIN' or guys in wife beaters reading 'Tell Your Boobs to Quit Starring at my Eyes' or 'I'm not Gay, but $20 bucks is $20 bucks", smoking cigars and drinking booze from paper bags. They all staggered around adding to the mob scene on Duval.

~ ~ ~

About a month before my ex-wife died, an old buddy of mine, Tom Finch from my accounting days, called to see if I had an interest in helping him raise money for a bar he was thinking of opening on the Rock. I laughed at the notion that he thought I had any money and although we chatted about his idea, I figured nothing would come of it.

Tom and I worked together in San Diego at the same accounting firm before I went into the Navy. We had sort of stayed in touch as guys do with periodic emails to catch up after I moved to Key West with Courtney and joined the KWPD. Before I married Courtney but after I got out of the Navy, I went back to my old firm and Tom was still there.

Over that year, we hung out again at the firm and during one particular weekend bender I shared with him that in the Navy I had acquired a nickname during SERE training.

SERE training is the fun thing that some of us *lucky chosen few* get to do as part of our warfare training. SERE stands for Survival, Evasion, Resistance and Escape. The whole point is to learn how to evade capture, develop survival skills and the military code of conduct. The U.S Air Force originally started it as military aircrews were the most likely to get captured. Now Special Forces also get trained as they are considered to be at risk in their covert operations.

So how I got my nickname was my middle name is Finnegan and I went by Finn. A smart-ass marine pilot decided to give me the call sign *Big Foot* and it stuck, at least through SERE.

One drunken night as we sat doing Tequila shooters at McPs on Coronado, Tom said with a distinct slur, "Finn, I mean, Big Foot, I want you to give me a cool call sign like you got at SERE. After all, I've been your wingman for the last year."

I paused for a minute. "Well OK," I said. "But once you get it regardless of whether you like it or not, you're stuck with it. Also, there is a tradition when you get a new call sign."

"Thas OK dude, I trus you," he mumbled and put his arm around me.

I ordered another round of shooters and climbed up on the bar yelling, "Listen up everyone." I paused for a second waiting for the place to quiet down and I continued loudly. "In keeping with long standing tradition, my buddy here and I have worked in the same accounting firm together for the last year and he wants to buy everyone in the house a round in celebration of his new call sign."

A loud cheer when up in the bar although they had no idea what I was talking about. "I would like you all to meet my wingman, Tom Finch, call sign, *Abacus*."

Silence fell over the crowd for a second, then one of the more literate patrons got it and started to laugh and cheer. Slowly as the drinks were served, some of the high school graduates who were still sober enough explained the sign to the less informed and many came over to Tom, slapped him on the back and bought him another drink calling him by his new name.

Responses included, "Abacus Finch. Great name, sure beats Boo," or "I think Scout would've been better but Abacus it is," etc.

By the time we staggered out and caught a cab, Tom was embracing his call sign and he has been Abacus ever since.

After almost ten years, Abacus called and said he was bored stiff with accounting and wanted to visit me in Key West.

He came down for a visit and we had a rowdy long weekend doing shooters of Tequila. Then three months ago, he called to see how I was doing after losing Courtney and again saying that he was ready to start our bar. Fast forward to my little inheritance and the next thing you know I'm his new partner, and no, not that kind of partner.

Chapter Four

SHORTLY AFTER my ex-wife's death, I received a note from her insurance company that I was the beneficiary of a two hundred and fifty thousand dollar policy from her estate. This was somewhat of a surprise given that we had been divorced for over three years, she had gotten me fired from the police department and she had tried to kill me. That was around the time of my *Square Grouper* adventure so now with the sudden windfall, I decided to invest the money.

I called Abacus and told him we should talk about the bar again. Six weeks later we were able to sub-lease a long-empty space on Duval near my place on Catherine Street and our new bar began to take shape. We kicked around a name for the place and after some reluctance and a few more shooters, he agreed the natural name for Key West's newest bar would be, the *Mockingbird*. It would specialize in Tequila.

I invested a hundred thousand of my windfall and for the past month we had been feverishly building out the interior including a bar shaped like the stern of a fishing boat name *Pilar*. Not only is it my last name, but also it was the name of Ernest Hemingway's favorite fishing boat when he lived in Key West. We figured this couldn't miss.

We stuck with a nautical theme for the interior with fishing nets, lobster traps and dive gear but the bar menu would be more Mexican. We were going to do Tacos, Burritos and Quesadillas but with Key West flair like Chipotle Key West Shrimp and Key Lime infused tortillas.

For those of you who have never constructed a bar, there are a million details to be worked out. Contractors in the Keys are notorious for over promising and under delivering so delays are inevitable. We were trying to do this on a shoestring so we could not afford to be paying rent for a long time while under construction and not producing revenue. I was the guy in charge of driving our schedule.

"Rico, what the hell is going on, or should I say not going on?" I yelled trying to be heard everywhere in the place. "Why am I looking at a pile of flooring and not a floor? And where the hell are the stainless wells for the bar bottles?" You get the idea.

Rico, our general contractor, came in through the swinging kitchen doors looking sheepish and said, "Oh Senor Finn, do not be upset. No worries we are still close to the plan and will have you open in two weeks. My best crew is going to be arriving tomorrow and we will be back on schedule in two days."

"Rico you have been telling me that for a week now and it is always manana, manana."

"Oh Senor Finn, it has been very challenging for me as well . . . Blah, blah, blah." You get the idea.

After way too long of this back and forth with Rico I had had enough and left to walk Crutch. I had about two hours before Stacy showed up and I needed to make progress on what had happened to Trixie. I picked up Crutch for his constitutional and we began walking along Whitehead toward the Southernmost Point.

As we sauntered along, I called OJ and to my surprise he picked up right away.

"Finn, where the hell have you been? I've been trying to reach you for an hour."

"Sorry dude, I had my phone off while working at the bar."

"I need to see you right away," he implored.

"I appreciate your bromance need to see me but I am currently engaged with Crutch in our inspection of trees and fences along Whitehead. Can it wait?"

"No," he said impatiently. "Meet me at your place in five minutes. Tell Crutch to cross his legs and get home."

"OJ, I may have to report you to the SPCA for violation of the Canines with Disabilities Act Rules for cruelty to disabled mutts."

Crutch looked up at me with a scowl. He hates to be thought of as disabled.

"Fuck off Finn, he's faster on three legs than most on four. Speaking of four, you're down to four minutes," and he hung up.

Crutch and I continued our leisurely stroll along Whitehead to the Southernmost Point, up South Street and back along Duval. We got back to my little conch cottage about ten minutes later all the while ignoring OJ's persistent calling over the last few minutes.

"You really are an asshole, Pilar!" OJ yelled as we walked up to the front gate.

I know he's really pissed when he calls me Pilar. "Come on OJ, Crutch needed some exercise to get things loosened up." Crutch looked up at me as if to say, "Thanks for throwing me under the bus Dad."

OJ took a deep breath and seemed to decide to let my tardiness go. He began, "Finn you have a problem. I know you were at Pussy Galore this afternoon. I saw you there and the bartender said you dropped off one of the girls just before the place blew up."

"Yeah, I was just doing a favor for a friend," I replied.

"Who was the girl? he asked "The one you dropped off?"

"Her name is Trixie, Trixie LaRue. At least that is what she calls herself," I said.

"Why was she with you?"

"OJ, what's this about and why do *I* have a problem? Remember it was *me* who called *you* offering any assistance I could because I was there when the explosion took place sitting in the parking lot waiting for Trixie."

"Why did you take off when I saw you?"

"OJ, I didn't take off when I saw you, although I guess you could look at it that way," I admitted. "When the bomb went off, I knew right away it was a bomb. I had heard way too many of them during my time in Iraq and Afghanistan," I offered. "I ran into the bar to see what had happened, looked into the locker room and immediately knew there was nothing I could do. I sat down in the bar to wait for the EMTs and Fire Department to show up. Once they arrived I figured there was nothing I could do but get in the way and I had things to do so I left."

OJ looked askance at me.

"Now you know what I know except for two things but I need something from you first," I proposed.

OJ looked at me for a minute then his face slowly turned red. "Listen you . . . you . . . you," he sputtered trying to gain control. He began his laundry list. "You are in no position to expect anything from me. You are a person of interest in this investigation. You were the last person to see the vic, and you have experience with explosives. You had opportunity and means so I just need to understand your motive."

I looked at him and laughed. "OJ, we worked together for eight years. You must be smokin' something to think I had anything to do with this. If you want to lock me up, go ahead but then I lawyer up and you may blow your only chance to solve this thing."

He looked like he wanted to throw me in the back of the squad car in hand cuffs and taser me.

"Listen dude, think for a minute. Whoever set off this bomb didn't care who was killed. This was an IED and the locker room could have been filled with a bunch of girls when it went off. Do you want my theory or not?" I waited.

He stopped, turned around in a circle once, twice then

a third time and replied, "OK, lay it on me."

"First of all, what's with the spinning around?" I asked.

"None of your fucking business!" he exclaimed.

"Come on dude, you have to admit, it's a pretty weird thing you just did."

He looked a little sheepish and replied, "My shrink tells me I have anger issues and if I feel like I am going to hit someone I should spin around to get control of my emotions."

"You have a shrink?" I chuckled. "Since when?"

"Fuck off Finn," and he started to spin again. I couldn't help but think of a Whirling Dervish.

"O.K. OJ, don't go all *Dancing with the Stars* on me." I continued much more seriously, "Look I dropped Trixie off at the club after picking her up when she was released from your offices this afternoon. She needed a change of clothes and said she had a paycheck at the club. I was waiting outside when the bomb went off."

"And?" he asked.

"I'm getting to it," I said slowly. "I was picking her up because her lawyer asked me to and her lawyer is Stacy." OJ knows Stacy and I are an item. "Stacy had filled me in on the situation and I was going to do a little detective work to help with the case. On the trip to the club I asked Trixie to tell me what happened with Rocco and she said she would tell me once we were back at my place."

"W . . .wait," he stammered. "You were taking Trixie to *your* place?"

"Yes. Stacy asked me to take her there to keep her safe."

"Safe from what?" he queried.

"Stacy didn't tell me and Trixie just said when I asked her on the ride to the club that she didn't know the other person in the room doing the filming."

OJ froze. "W . . .wait," he stammered once again.

I was beginning to worry about this new way of

speaking to me.

"There was another person in the room making a video when she shot Rocco?"

"Allegedly shot Rocco," I reminded OJ. "And I know, I almost drove off the road when she said it."

OJ paused, took a breath then said, "So you're telling me Rocco and Trixie were having sex in her trailer, smoking meth and playing Russian roulette while someone else in the room was filming it? Jesus," he muttered. "This is getting really kinky. Where the hell is the video? And who was doing the filming?"

Both good questions we need to figure out.

"Trixie said she needed the money and figured no big deal. She had really gone downhill since I last saw her a few months ago. We both know meth will really fuck you up."

"So what do you want from me?" he asked.

"OK, so this is how I see it," I began. "Based on what I saw in the club locker room, whoever was in there was vaporized. Correct?"

"Basically yeah. We are going to have to use DNA to identify the victim," he offered.

"Makes sense." I suggested, "It's possible that it was not Trixie, correct?"

"W . . .wait, what?" There he goes again. Now I am really starting to worry.

"Well it *is* possible. Both the bartender and I saw her go in and didn't see her come out so it's a safe bet it was her but it may also not have been her."

"OK it's possible that she left through the back door without either of you seeing her."

"So here is the ask." I paused for effect. "Suppose we say that two girls were in the locker room according to witnesses but that only one body was found and is being identified. The second girl was injured and is under police guard at Lower Keys Medical."

"What are you getting at Finn?"

"Whoever placed that bomb was probably trying to kill Trixie and didn't care who else got hurt. Assuming it's a he, he is really dangerous and will stop at nothing. He is going to want to make sure it was Trixie who was killed so he will need to find out who was only injured. That gives us a chance to catch him."

I watched as OJ's mental gears ground through the idea for a minute then he said, "Ok let me talk to the Chief and see if he'll go along with the possibility. We will not release any DNA test results and I will take the bartender in for questioning. That should keep this quiet for at least twenty-four hours."

With that he walked back to his car, turned and said. "No cracks about the shrink asshole, or next time I twirl it will be on your head."

I laughed as he drove off, then I ran into the house for a quick shower and headed to the airport to pick up Stacy.

~ ~ ~

As I rode to the airport with Crutch riding shotgun on the floorboards of the scooter, I thought about seeing Stacy. In the spirit of full disclosure, I knew Stacy was going to be pissed at *me* but she loves Crutch, so coward that I am I hoped she might soften a bit with him by my side.

My phone app, FlightAware, told me she was in the air from Tampa and about ten minutes out when we pulled into the scooter parking area. The Key West Airport is small (although checked luggage takes forever to travel the few hundred feet from plane to one of the two baggage conveyor belts). Although the current terminal boasts of two gates, there is really only one that people actually come through so it's pretty easy to meet someone. There is a small kiosk bar beside the gate entrance so I ordered a Bud Light for Crutch and a Stella for me as we waited.

We were sitting in the truly uncomfortable airport

waiting area stools enjoying our beers when Stacy came storming in. First off the plane and with a head of steam, she glanced around and then saw me then Crutch side-by-side nursing our beers.

Ignoring me, she accepted a big doggy beer breath slobber from Crutch, then whispered, "You are such a coward, Finn, trying to soften me up by bringing your sidekick with you."

"Man's best friend, babe," I said with what I hoped was a charming boyish grin to win her over.

~ ~ ~

"Don't give me that pathetic Finn Pilar boyish grin crap," she spit out. "You are in deep shit with me. Now let's get out of here so I can truly tell you how I feel," and she stomped out of the arrivals area toward the parking lot.

As I headed for the scooter lot she stopped. "You have got to be kidding me." She turned and leered at me. "You expect me to ride on the scooter with you and Crutch after you've both been drinking?"

"It was only one beer, babe," I said sheepishly. *Boy, was she hot, and she was pissed too. I can be a real wus when I want to get laid.*

She immediately turned and walked over to the taxi cabstand in front of the terminal. One of the local cabbies practically stumbled over himself to open her door. Beautiful women everywhere get the best treatment from cabbies. She threw her bag in the trunk and pointed to Crutch.

"Take the dog to Catherine and Duval" she growled as she gave him twenty bucks. "I'm going with this asshole and will meet you there if we both make it alive."

Crutch jumped in the back and lay down on the seat before the cabbie changed his mind. "So much for man's best friend," I said but he just farted and closed his eyes for the ride. There are some things in this world you can always count on.

Stacy stomped over to the scooter, put her hand out for the key and fired it up. "You can get on or catch another cab. Make up your mind."

Completely cowed - *read still hoping for a little nooky* - I considered the cab, then again wimped and hopped on the jump seat. "Stacy, I know you're pissed but you need to listen to me," I implored.

"Finn, how could you let this happen? Trixie was in trouble and you were supposed to protect her."

"Stacy, when you called me, all you asked was that I pick her up when she was released and take her back to my place. You didn't suggest that she was in danger or that I needed to protect her."

"Finn you're an ex-cop and you should have known that she was at risk." Her voice began to break. Suddenly this show began to make sense. "Stacy, pull over," and she did.

I got off the scooter and helped her off, putting it up on its stand. "Stacy, listen to me. It is not your fault that this happened. You had no way of knowing that she was in any danger and neither did I."

She burst into tears.

What the hell is going on?

"Stacy," I softened my voice the best I could. "Is there something you are not telling me?" I asked. It didn't take a rocket scientist or a psych major to tell that I did not have all the information to know what the hell was going on with her.

"Finn, I . . . I . . . I . . ." and she burst again into tears.

This might take all day I thought impatiently but I asked her gently, "Babe, what is it?"

She took a deep breath, let it out slowly and began again.

"Finn, I . . . ." She paused, pulled it together and started again. "I should have known by the way Trixie seemed so scared, really frightened. I put it down to being in lock up and feeling alone with a serious potential charge hanging over her."

"Stacy stop." I said in my most commanding voice. "There is no way you could have known this would happen." I just couldn't bear seeing tears again.

"Finn, she told me there was something else that she needed to tell me but it could wait till she saw me in person. She wouldn't say anything more even though I pushed. Maybe if I had pushed harder or tried to get here quicker . . . " Stacy paused. "I should have at least told you that something more was going on and you might have been able to learn what it was."

Oh shit I thought. I decided to come clean.

"Stacy, as we were going to the club after I picked Trixie up, she told me something that I knew was important but it didn't register with me as immediately dangerous. I should have at least taken precautions although in the end we would probably both be dead.

Trixie, told me that there was someone else in the room filming the sex/drugs/dumb-shit Russian roulette thing. It never occurred to me that it was so serious that they would kill her over it, at least until now. I'm so sorry."

Stacy just looked at me and simply said, "You are right Finn. We both let her down."

That is not exactly what I said but being the loving and supportive guy that I am, I agreed. Well actually, if I had any chance of enjoying a *debrief* tonight, I'd better agree. *Even I know that much.*

"Finn, we better get back to the house. Crutch is probably waiting and we need to figure out what to do next."

We hopped on the scooter and rode the rest of the way home in silence. As we pulled up, we could see Crutch sitting beside Stacy's roller bag guarding it from a couple of homeless guys hovering near by eyeing it.

I walked over to the corner, slipped the homeless guys a couple of bucks each and thanked them for guarding the bag and the dog. Hey, it's Key West after all; that's what we do. There but for the grace of a few bad choices or bad luck go any of us.

As Stacy unpacked, then grabbed a shower, I mixed a couple of Dark and Stormys and threw some bacon wrapped shrimp rolled in brown sugar and chili powder in the oven.

Sitting on the back deck waiting for Stacy and enjoying the rustle of the overhead palm fronds and music wafting from La Te Da, I began to think about my plan to catch the *Pussy Club Bomber*. Suddenly my stomach did a couple of back flips.

Chapter Five

TO NOBODY IN PARTICULAR, I muttered, "How did the bomber know that Trixie would go to the club after her release? Or did he even know when she was to be released?"

Bombers are indiscriminate killers. In Afghanistan they didn't just place IEDs on the main roads but even the least likely roads into and out of FOBs. A Forward Operating Base is a secured military position, generally a military base that is used to support whatever operations are needed in that area. It might be a landing strip or a hospital.

Could this guy have put more bombs in places Trixie was likely to go?

Jumping up from my comfortable position on the outdoor sofa, I ran for my phone. "OJ!" I yelled when he picked up."

"Quit yelling Finn. I can hear you just fine."

I shouted, "SHUT THE FUCK UP and listen. Have you or your team been over to Trixie's place on Stock since the club bombing?"

"I just sent a couple of guys over there about ten minutes ago to. . . . "

I cut him off yelling again, "Stop them NOW and don't let anyone in the place. It may be wired to blow like the club. I am on my way." I hung up.

How could I have missed this and what other places could be wired?

I ran into the house calling out to Stacy, "I'm an idiot. I've been thinking of nothing but getting you in the sack and now I may have killed someone in the process."

She stepped out of the shower looking stunning in a towel and also stunned by my tirade.

"Take the shrimp out of the oven in twenty minutes and don't wait up. I hope I'm not too late," And out I ran.

I fired up the scooter and tore the wrong way up Catherine. Well tore is relative but as fast as the scooter would go. Stock Island is about five miles from where I live but usually about a fifteen-minute drive with tourists, traffic and speed limits. I ignored all three and made it in eight flat.

As I screamed over Cow Key Bridge, I saw a stream of emergency vehicles with lights flashing and sirens blaring and followed them, not knowing exactly where Trixie lived.

As I pulled up, I could see OJ directing vehicles to stay about a hundred yards away from one trailer and cops going door to door around it clearing out the unhappy people. Yellow tape was being strung to create a wide perimeter as I ran up to OJ.

"OK Finn, I have done what you ask but you better explain what the hell this is about."

I talked fast to bring OJ up to speed. "The bomb that went off at Pussy Galore must have been planted before Trixie asked me to take her there. So how did the bomber know to put it there? He probably made the assumption that she would go there after being released and obviously not caring who else got hurt. The question I missed was, where else might she have gone after her release and a safe bet is her trailer. I would bet there is a bomb in there."

"Jesus Finn." He paused, then asked, "OK so now what? You know we don't have a bomb squad in Key West and need to call Miami which will take some time to get here" He paused again and looked at me.

Great, my past comes back to haunt me again. After I dropped out of the SEAL's BUD/S training with a blown knee and after six months of rehab, I joined the EOD program and eventually did tours in Iraq and Afghanistan. EOD is Explosive Ordinance Disposal. Now OJ was looking for me to take on this little project.

"OJ, look. This is not your usual EOD task," I pointed out.

"What? A bomb is a bomb," he said matter-of-factly.

"Listen man, most of what we did was simply clear an area around a bomb, remote detonate the IED and then figure out the trigger to find the bomb maker and kill him with a sniper. The rest is just movie stuff."

OJ stared at me then said, "Well we can't just detonate this trailer on spec that you think there might be a bomb in it. It could take out all these other trailers as well. You need to help us," he implored.

"Dude, it is not that simple. Look, a bomb is a bomb at least in general terms; the challenge is the triggers and here you have three or at least derivations of three. One is a pin type like a grenade. You pull the pin and with some amount of delay it blows. The second type is a timer that is set for a particular time or amount of time, then it blows. Finally there can be a remote detonation like a cell phone or a garage door opener that goes off when the bomber wants to set it off."

"OK Mr. Google, so what?"

I thought back to the club bomb and said, "If you think of the bomb at the club, it was probably a pin type. The act of opening the locker, pulls the pin. The bomber couldn't tell when she would be there so timers wouldn't work. A remote would require him to be in the area and be able to see Trixie go in and when the locker would be opened. Again unlikely."

As I described the different scenarios, I could feel my mouth drying out and my stomach roiling. "If this one is a pin type like a grenade or a land mine, it could be anywhere in the trailer. You could step on a stair, open a door, a cupboard, the fridge, or lift a toilet seat and set it off."

"Jesus, Finn, now what?"

OK, so the last thing I wanted to do was start wandering around this trailer lifting the toilet seat. That could be bad even with no bomb.

"Your best bet is a bomb sniffing dog to see if there are any signs of explosives in the trailer but given that this is where Rocco got shot and it's most likely his meth lab, there are probably lots of different elements or compounds that may be similar to bomb making chemicals. If I were you, I would call Miami, tell them what you may have then seal off the area till they get here. In the meantime try to get a chemical analysis of the bomb at the club so when the dog gets here it can at least have a scent to follow."

The KWPD began to string lights up around the trailer that Rocco and Trixie used for their film making endeavors. We were all just standing around watching so I suggested to OJ that I go to Pussy's to see if I could learn anything from the earlier explosion. I needed to see if there was anything that might give me an idea regarding the rig etc. In my experience bombers usually follow a pattern and develop a *signature* that can help with identification.

As I walked back to the security line, the explosion rocked me off my feet and sent debris blowing in all directions. I rolled back in time to see the roof of the trailer landing back onto the foundation now that the walls were collapsed. I struggled to get my bearings and staggered to my feet.

Many of the half dozen or so cops that had been around the trailer were now on the ground either groaning or worse, unnaturally silent. I rushed back to find OJ struggling to get up but his leg was bleeding badly and he appeared to have been hit by debris from the side panels of the house.

I pulled my belt from my shorts and quickly wrapped it around his thigh to slow the bleeding and called out for a medic. I meant an EMT but old habits come back quickly and un-filtered. OJ's eyes came into focus and he looked down to see that while he was in one piece, he would not be doing cartwheels any time soon. Not that he could even do them before as far as I knew.

"What the fuck happened?" he asked looking around with bulging eyes.

"Well," I proposed, "Either someone was in the trailer and they set off the bomb by accident or our unsub used a timer or remote detonation. Until I can get in and we sift through the wreckage, we can't tell."

I continued assessing OJ's injury. "Look OJ, you are down for the count for at least the next twenty-four hours so let the EMTs take you to the ER and I will see what I can learn from the two bombings so far."

OJ faded to semi consciousness while one of the EMTs came over with a gurney, gave him a quick examination, checked the tourniquet, put him on a saline drip with some morphine and ordered him taken to the Lower Keys Medical for treatment and observation. *So much for my favorite belt, now soaked in blood wrapped around his leg.*

As they carried him away, it was clear the explosion and fire had destroyed most of the trailer and a couple of the surrounding ones as well. Having to wait until the ruined trailer was cool enough to examine for evidence, I called Stacy brought her up to speed and said I would head home after a stop at Pussy Galore.

"What, you don't think you have enough back here?" she pouted. "You have to go over there looking?"

"Babe, make a reservation at Martin's and I will meet you there. Order me a Sunset Martini and I'll see you in forty-five minutes."

Stacy's voice took on a sultry tone as she said, "Why don't I just throw a couple of steaks on the grill, open a bottle of your favorite LA Cietto Cab and I'll make you a *Naked Sunset.*"

"What's a . . . . ? Never mind, I'll be there in thirty minutes," I said as I hung up.

~ ~ ~

A scooter is a great way to get around Key West and popular with both locals and tourists alike. It's easy to get around traffic and to park almost anywhere. The only drawback is if you are in a real hurry to get somewhere, it takes a bit longer than a car as you can only go so fast.

I raced down from Stock Island onto North Roosevelt, across the Palm Avenue Bridge and down Eaton to Pussy Galore. To my surprise, the parking lot was full and it was impossible to miss the clearly rushed hand painted signs, *Our girls are really hot* and *They will blow your .... mind.* A little too soon I thought, but the guys who run these places aren't known for being PC.

The bar was hopping, a naked girl gyrating on stage and several half naked ones doing lap dances in the darker corners of the place. The fire damage by the girl's locker room was hidden by a couple of hastily strung up sheets. There was an odor combination of smoke and cheap perfume which on reflection was probably normal given the clientele.

The music pounded while a well-endowed, clearly bleached blonde with a mole between her breasts did her best to move with the beat. *OK, so I notice things like when the drapes don't match the carpet. I was a cop after all.*

The vacant look in her eyes spoke volumes regarding her level of enthusiasm for the activity. Something told me she was not only bored but also anxious to get off the main stage. The crowd was mostly local shrimpers back from a few days at sea, a smattering of off duty navy guys, and a drunken bachelor party trying to get the apparent groom on stage with the girl. A typical night I surmised.

I walked up to the bartender who recognized me, and no not because I'm a regular, but from seeing me earlier in the day. I asked him if I could go to the back and he just shrugged and went back to rinsing glasses in steaming water. I was surprised as I hadn't expected a place like this to care too much about health department rules.

Behind the curtain it was clear that once the fire was put out nothing had yet been done to clean up the mess. The entire locker room was badly charred. In addition to the smell of smoke, it was beginning to smell of decay because of the bits of leftover body tissue on the walls. Whoever was in here, if it wasn't Trixie, had no idea what hit them.

The lockers were against the left wall, mostly bent and charred. It was clear that one in particular was completely destroyed and had been the center of the blast. Its door was hanging by a single hinge at the top and blown half off on the bottom. They were half size lockers like the ones from my old high school and each showed a tattered remnant of paper card with a dancer's name on it. A few had locks but most did not.

Looking inside the locker that was probably Trixie's, whatever had been there was completely vaporized. The traces along the inside showed charring and most immediately evidence of shrapnel.

What killed her could have been as simple as a grenade fixed to the bottom of the locker with duct tape and a string attached to the pin. When the locker opened, the pin was pulled and as Trixie looked inside, the grenade blew up. The explosive force from that distance would have killed her instantly.

More detailed forensic tests would answer some of my burning questions but this preliminary observation told me this was not a sophisticated bomb maker who did this. It could have been any local bozo with access to a grenade, which in Florida you can find at any gun show along with a fifty Caliber sniper rifle, Teflon coated armor piercing bullets or an AK 47 with a thirty round magazine.

In some ways I was hoping for something a little more complex which would have narrowed the possible suspects but now the pool was just about anybody. Shit.

I checked my watch and realized I was going to have to really sprint to make it for the steaks so they wouldn't be burnt offerings. *Like that was my priority.*

~ ~ ~

As I pulled up to the house, I could smell the steaks charring on the barbeque. As I walked down the side of the house I could hear Zac Brown playing *Knee Deep* from the speakers on the deck. I paused for a second to take it in. I turned the corner to see Stacy in the kitchen with a salad bowl and a martini in hand coming out to the deck singing along to the words.

> *Wishin' I was*
> *Knee deep in the water somewhere*
> *Got the blue sky, breeze and it don't seem fair*
> *The only worry in the world*
> *Is the tide gonna reach my chair.*
> *Sunrise, there's a fire in the sky*
> *Never been so happy*
> *Never felt so high*

And I think I might have found me my own kind of paradise."

She smiled when she saw me, planted a chaste kiss on my cheek and said, "The steaks will be ready in seven minutes so go take a shower while the Cab is breathing." She handed me the martini and turned to flip the steaks.

I think I have found my own kind of paradise.

I took a quick shower to wash off the smoke, blood and grime from the crime scenes. I changed out of my blood stained shirt and shorts into my third and last pair of shorts and my favorite long sleeved yellow linen shirt.

52

I tossed back the remainder of the martini as I walked out to the deck. Tracy lay lounging on the L-shaped sofa wearing a silky Technicolor dream kimono tied loosely at her waist and creeping up her thigh. If the steaks were not resting on the side table with the salad waiting for the blue cheese dressing beside them, I might have simply ravaged her on the spot.

Instead as the model of self-restraint, I gallantly said, "Will they keep?" and moved toward her beginning to remove my linen shirt.

"Hold on big boy. I'm famished and still pissed at you that Trixie was not better protected." She paused, and added sadly, "By us both." For a moment I thought she was going to begin crying again but she caught herself and continued, "While we eat, tell me what happened when you went racing out of here."

She poured a glass of the wine that I had picked up on a visit to the L.A. Cetto winery in Guadalupe Valley in Baja, California. Cetto was the fourth winery built in Mexico and has been making wonderful wines since 1928. We tasted it, savoring the hints of licorice and chocolate, then tucked into the salad and steak. Actually I never could taste all the stuff the wine snobs claim to taste but I know what I like.

I brought her up to speed perhaps embellishing my heroics at the scene just a little bit. "OJ was walking away from the trailer and when the explosion happened, I jumped on him to protect him as the debris came crashing down around us." Actually that's what I might have said if I were not an Eagle Scout so I gave her the summary of the actual events.

"When we got home, I had a panic attack that the other place Trixie might have asked to go would be her trailer. If the bomber wanted to be sure to get her out of the picture, he could not have been sure she would go to the club. He would need to have a way to get her at home. I was afraid the cops would go to her trailer to go over it next and if there was another bomb intended for Trixie then the cops might get hurt."

I was hoping the look in her eyes at my reasoning skills would transfer soon to my other skills. "It turned out I was right. While we were clearing the area and waiting for the bomb-sniffing dog from Miami to come down, the trailer blew up. Several cops were hurt but thankfully none killed. Until the scene cools off, we can't go in to figure out what happened; hence I am here having a wonderful evening with you." I smiled my most boyish smile.

I took a breath, paused and stuffed another slice of perfectly cooked New York strip in my mouth with another sip of wine. Crutch who had been bouncing beside me on his three legs in anticipation of some meat finally put on his *sad face, where is mine, hang dog* whimper and I cut a good sized chunk for him. He did his back flip and inhaled the steak.

"So what's next?" asked Stacy and I leered at her.

"Not what I meant; let me rephrase. Where do you go from here with the case?" she asked.

"Well with the trailer destroyed, I am going to have to start talking to witnesses, the bartender for example and the other dancers at the club to see if they saw anything suspicious or if they had been approached about making porn videos."

"Sounds like a really tough assignment," she grinned, "Perhaps we should work on your interrogation techniques." She slowly untied the sash from her robe and let it fall across her leg. "Do you tie up your suspects?" she asked.

I leaned over and gently kissed her. She returned the kiss and soon we were in a tangle of legs, linen and lust on the L-shaped sofa. I had been torn between buying a dining table and chairs for al fresco dining or a sofa for the back deck. *Am I ever happy I choose the latter?*

She came up for air and said flirtatiously, "Wait, I promised you a naked Sunset Martini. Go lie down on the bed and I will be right in."

I couldn't toss Crutch the remains of my steak fast enough before I walked awkwardly into the bedroom taking my shorts off as I went. I lay naked on the bed in anticipation of what was about to unfold when she came into the room with a martini glass filled with whip cream and my old hand cuffs from the kitchen drawer.

"OK big boy, lie back and put your arms above your head," she demanded. She proceeded to tie my right hand to one bedpost with the sash from her kimono and my left to the bedpost with the cuffs. At the sound of the cuffs, I could see Crutch crawl under the throw pillows on the sofa to cover his ears.

Stacy has always been comfortable being naked and I was reminded why as she leaned over to tie me up staying just out of reach. Her tan was even and complete without the hint of a tan line. Her figure was perfection from the curve of her breasts to the mold of her butt with a tiny waist in between. I tried to sit up to reach a nipple with my mouth but she nimbly dodged away.

She knelt between my legs and smiled while admiring her handiwork. My hands may have been tied down but my important bits were clearly not.

She took a finger of whipped cream from the martini glass and put it in my mouth. Then she put one in hers. Finally, she slowly and sensuously dipped a finger in the glass and put it on each of her nipples for me to lick off. Her skin took on a warm pink tone while she then put whip cream on each of my now erect nipples and the other very erect appendage.

"OK" she purred in a husky tone, "It's time for the sunset." And the sun went down.

Thus began our reunion.

At one point in my life, we might still have been entangled as the sun rose. Stacy is a free spirited, uninhibited and energetic lover and she rode this ole train until I ran out of track. I collapsed into a deep sleep and awoke to pounding at my door.

Chapter Six

"GOD WHAT TIME IS IT?" I asked groggily as I opened the door to Abacus.

"Dude it's eight thirty and Rico has not shown up yet." He was clearly in a panic. "If we don't get opened in the next two weeks we may never open. We are hemorrhaging cash and we need to get generating revenue." He stopped short. "Oh, sorry I didn't realize you had company," he gasped as he looked over my shoulder to see Stacy standing framed by the door to the bedroom in her kimono. The kimono was a little transparent and the sun backlit her frame, offering a hint of the sights beneath.

She waved to Abacus and walked into the kitchen to make coffee. His eyes followed her until I stepped between them and directed him to the outside.

The remnants of our dinner lay strewn on the coffee table and my linen shirt lay crumpled in a heap on the deck. It was pretty clear why we were still sleeping.

I spent the next five minutes talking Abacus off the ledge from his meltdown. "Look, we spent a lot of time selecting Rico for the job because every reference we checked said he finished on time and on budget. If he says he will have us open, he will."

What Abacus didn't know, was that I had a back up plan in the event that Rico was late.

During my police days I had been hired for security several times by a Mexican tequila baron from Guadalajara, Ricardo Ramos. Ricardo was a seventh generation tequila maker whose family owned a large agave plantation outside of Guadalajara. We first met when I was in EOD doing contract work. Every year he would hire me to act as the

Tequila Mockingbird

liaison between his personal security team and the Key West police. He and his family came to Key West from Miami several times a year for either deep sea fishing or the Power Boat races.

Key West hosts an annual Offshore Power Boat World Championship race that takes place off Mallory Square between Key West and Sunset Key. These are the huge offshore speedboats that reach speeds over a hundred miles an hour.

His Tequila company, *Azul Primero,* sponsors an unlimited class boat the *Agave Thunder* that is rumored to be fueled by his company's tequila, *Reposado Negro.* While they denied the rumor, I've on more than one occasion while escorting his group around the docks, seen him pour a shot of it into the fuel tanks. "For luck," he said with a winning smile. "Besides, it's a bio fuel."

We remained friends even after I left the force and when I told him about our idea for a tequila bar in Key West he was very excited and offered to invest. I said that until I had a better idea what the numbers looked like, I would just take advantage of his knowledge of tequila to help with selecting what we offered in the bar. He agreed but said he was still interested in investing.

I knew that for a reasonable percentage of the business we could get all the funding we needed but I wanted to try and get it done on a shoe string. Key West eats new restaurants up - pun intended - and I valued his friendship more that his money.

I called Rico and got voicemail. "Morning sleepy head," I said. "I thought we were going to have breakfast this morning and talk about the plan to get things finished up in the next two weeks." It was a little white lie but rather than get pissed I sometimes find guilt, even though misleading, can be more effective with him. "Call me when you get this and we can reschedule."

One of the things I have learned about contractors in Key West is they are always looking for the next job. As they work toward finishing one job, they are trying to manage their crews so they start the next job even before the last one is finished. This way they don't lose the crew for lack of work. To keep a contractor working on your job to the end, you need to have a clear plan and stay on him or her. You also need to hold back payments until the job is fully complete.

With Abacus mollified, I returned to the kitchen to find Stacy with a blender full of something green. "It's a little early for a green Bloody Mary Stacy, even for me," I observed. "I was going to suggest we go over to La Te Da for the Eggs Blackstone and Mimosas."

She scowled and looked like she was about to say something like, "That is disgusting. It's full of fat and will add at least two inches to my waistline. How will you feel about me if I'm fat?"

Instead she said, "OK, I'll put this in the fridge and we can go for a swim after breakfast. We can race to the buoy and back twice and you skip your morning Bloody."

I looked at her and almost took the pitcher of green stuff. *Almost.*

By the time we finished breakfast and our swim, I was ready for a nap. When we got back to the house she slipped out of her suit and leered at me as she slipped beneath the sheets. I followed and we napped.

This girl is an amazing nap taker.

As I lay in bed completely exhausted, the phone beside me began to ring. Hoping it was Rico I decided to take the call.

"Finn, where the fuck have you been? I've been trying to reach you for hours," OJ said. "We need to talk."

"I've been napping," I responded with a smile in my voice.

"Napping? Napping? What are you, sixty?" he snapped. "You need to get yourself over Stock Island to look at what we found at Trixie's place. You may have a problem."

I paused, "Why would *I* have a problem?"

"When you see the body we found in the trailer, or the pieces of body, you'll understand. Now get your ass up here, yesterday!" and he hung up.

Stacy was now awake beside me showing no interest in moving. I reached over and kissed her and she pulled me closer pressing herself against me. *I could feel another nap coming on.* Well maybe stirrings, but I am coming up on forty and stirrings was about all I could produce at this point. I needed some more recovery time. With regret, I rolled away and said, "Can we take this up again later? I need some of that green energy stuff and some time. Besides, OJ wants me to look at a body they found in Trixie's trailer."

"Whose body?" she asked as she stepped out of bed and reached for that beguiling kimono.

I was beginning to regret my decision when she stood briefly and put the kimono on. I turned away and said, "Not sure but OJ sure seem excited. Why don't you hang here for the day?" and looking down at her I leered, "We can pick this up later."

She smiled and purred, "I am ready whenever you are big boy." I took a deep breath and sighed.

"Can't wait," she continued, and walked out of the room into the shower.

How did I ever get this lucky?

Meanwhile, Crutch was sitting cross-legged by the door looking pissed having not peed or eaten since we went to breakfast almost four hours ago. *That had been a long nap.*

"Sorry Crutch," I apologized. Let's take you for a quick one and then you can come up to Stock with me. Crutch loves to ride with me on the floorboards of the scooter so he

60

seemed to perk up and ate while I got dressed.

Stacy came out of the shower looking demur in her robe, gave me a peck on the cheek and blew a kiss to Crutch. "You boys drive safe now and I'll see you both later," she said as she sauntered seductively into the bedroom to change and Crutch and I headed out for Stock Island.

~ ~ ~

The afternoon heat was at its peak and the humidity felt like steam from a hot shower. It reminded me of when I was a kid. My mom would fill a bowl with hot water and I would bend over it with a towel over my head and breathe in the steam to open up my congested lungs when I had a cold.

Even the breeze as I rode up North Roosevelt toward Stock Island didn't cool the sweat and my shirt stuck to me like a damp paper towel. Even Crutch was beginning to regret this ride as he panted on the floorboards of the scooter.

We pulled up to the tired looking trailer park that seemed like a resting place for trailers built in the forty's. The only green around the place were clumps of sage grass growing between cracks in what must at one time have been asphalt parking spots. The trailers themselves were more rust than paint with leaking window air conditioners wheezing and grinding in an attempt to cool the interior of these *Easy Bake* tin ovens.

The explosion the previous evening still emitted tendrils of smoke from a couple of hot spots beneath the rubble but fire crews had pretty much doused them. The remnants of the trailer had begun to cool as much as it could in the ninety-degree heat and detectives were sifting through the damage searching for clues to the explosion.

Crutch and I sauntered over to OJ who was talking to another detective I had run into during an earlier case.

"Hey asshole!" he called out to me.

"Back at you, Donnelly. If I had known you were going

to be here I would have brought you some breath mints," I replied sarcastically.

He took a step toward me and OJ grabbed his arm.

"Fuck you Finn. Just because OJ was your former partner doesn't cut slack with me. You are still a wife beater in my book and you got off too easy."

Our running battle is a longer story as he and I had the *pleasure* of working with each other on multiple cases when I was a cop. Once I left the force, he wanted to charge me in the death of a Bubba, the local's name for influential Key West-born movers and shakers. For all its charm and international reputation, at one level Key West is just like any small town in America with a handful of longtime residents who imagine they have power and influence when in reality most of us don't really give a shit about them. They are the big fish in a very tiny pond.

Rather than engage any more with Donnelly I said, "OJ, I suggest we talk about this case at least twenty feet from Donnelly so I can breathe. His breath has not improved since our last encounter." *OK, so I am not very diplomatic.*

Donnelly pulled loose from OJ's grip on his arm and charged toward me. In his rage he missed the fact that I was standing with a big slab of twisted, rusty trailer siding in front of me. When he stepped on it he tumbled on his ass in a jumble of arms, legs and trailer parts cursing me as he fell. OJ swung around him and grabbed him again.

"Donnelly!" shouted OJ. "Give it up and get back to work. I told you to get the DNA sample down to the lab and see if you can find a match. And you Finn, quit jerking his chain and come with me."

Donnelly rose from the rubble looking like he was ready to beat me to a pulp but seemed to realize now was not the best time. After dusting himself off, he walked away cursing me as he went.

"Next time motherfucker . . . " he mumbled under his

rancid breath. "And a good day to you too detective," I smiled. I have always loved nurturing my friendships.

"Jesus Finn, you can be such an asshole," steamed OJ as we walked together toward a spot on the other side of what used to be a trailer.

I quietly apologized then got on my high horse again. "Donnelly is a foul mouthed prick in the true sense of the phrase." *So I'm not so good at giving an apology.*

"I should have reminded you to bring the Tic-Tacs," OJ chuckled.

His look turned serious as we walked up to a black shiny tarp on the ground. "Finn, I am going to need your help. This morning once the trailer had cooled, we began searching the wreckage and found this."

He gingerly lifted the tarp like a magician pulling a handkerchief off a top hat to reveal a rabbit. *All I could think of was, ta-da!*

Chapter Seven

BENEATH THE TARP were a bunch of body parts clearly blown up during the explosion and gathered together like jigsaw puzzle pieces dumped for the first time from a box.

"Damn OJ, you could have warned me," I sputtered. Now this is not the first time I had seen body parts after an explosion; in fact, during my tours in Iraq and Afghanistan I had seen too many. It was the context that bothered me. Key West is in America and bomb victims are rare.

Also, I recognized the body. *Shit, this is not good.*

OJ continued, "I know you have a lot of experience with this kind of thing so I am interested in your take on the type of explosive used in this bombing."

My mind was racing. Do I tell him I recognize the body to save him a lot of trouble trying to identify it or do I let him swing in the wind while I try to sort this out first?

Being the upstanding citizen that I am, I punted. "Dude, two things," I began as I bought time.

"The bomb at the club was a simple grenade rigged to explode when the locker was opened. This one seems to be different as there are no shrapnel wounds or grenade fragments in the body parts," I began. "I will need to look around more for the trigger and do some chemical tests but this is a much more sophisticated bomb."

"And the second thing?" OJ asked.

"Have you identified the body?"

OJ looked at me as if to say, "What are you blind? These are just bits and pieces!"

I paused, took a breath and said, "I may know who it is."

OJ looked surprised.

"Yesterday, I was looking into the arrest of Trixie after being asked by her lawyer to help with the case," I began. "During the course of my enquiries, I became aware of an individual who might have information regarding the circumstances of the death of Rocco Ramon. During my conversation with said individual, I noticed something that seems familiar with this victim."

"Finn, cut the cop speak bullshit and tell me who it is," OJ said impatiently.

"Squeaky MacKay."

"Shit Finn, how can you tell?" asked OJ.

"When I talked to Squeaky before the bombing at the club, he was drunk as usual. During questioning, he puked on my sandals and on his own shoes. He was wearing the same red sneakers as the foot and shoe in your pile of parts here."

OJ looked down at the pile and a scorched red Converse sneaker was still laced on the foot of what remained of the lower half of a right leg.

"Alright Finn, let's start from the beginning."

I walked him through the call from Stacy, my meeting with Billy and then finding Squeaky at the Wharf. I skipped the threats I used with Squeaky and simply said we had a chat over a lunch. It was sort of true; after all it *was* during the lunch hour and I *had* ordered lunch. OJ knew me well enough to suspect I was leaving out stuff.

"So what the hell was he doing here?" he asked.

"What, like I should know? Your guess is as good as mine. Maybe he was looking for meth and got more than he bargained for."

While OJ was processing this, I reflected on Trixie's comment about the videotaping session at the trailer. I wondered if Squeaky was the third person in the room when Rocco took his last shot, so to speak. Could Squeaky have been looking for the tape or tapes? I needed to get a look at

66

what was found at the site to find both the bomb trigger and any tapes.

"OJ, I would like to look around the site for the bomb trigger. Any problem with that? I asked.

"Knock yourself out Finn. None of my guys have any background in this stuff," he said.

~ ~ ~

My tours in Iraq and Afghanistan as an EOD specialist had given me an unusually useful qualification in this situation. After I med dropped out of the Navy SEAL's BUD/S program, I was given the option of getting into Explosive Ordinance Disposal (EOD) training once I was healthy. After two tours in the *Suck* I decided that *old* EOD guys were rare so I got out, but not before getting exposure to almost every type of IED Al-Qaeda and the Taliban could come up with.

As I began to deliberately walk the scene, Crutch sat patiently by the scooter. I was looking for the center of the explosion. Debris spreads out from the center of a detonation so you can begin walking a debris field as it radiates out. Slow circles around the center can reveal the power of the explosive and with luck you can find a trigger. It can be as simple as a switch that releases or as complex as a cell phone or garage door electrical charge setting off the explosion by a person nearby pressing a button or by timer.

After about twenty minutes, Crutch got bored and to give himself a natural high, went looking for a neighborhood pit bull to sniff. I continued to walk. Round and round in ever-larger circles. Something was strange. It seemed that this blast was centered in mid air with a blast pattern blowing down and out.

With the roof of the trailer gone I could only surmise that the blast started about four to five feet up from the floor in the middle of what looked like the bedroom. Bits of mattress were burned but visible and some metal spikes appeared to be driven into the remains of the floor. I called OJ over.

"Dude, take a look at this," I said pointing to the spikes and the mattress. He looked for a minute then said, "OK Sherlock, what am I supposed to be looking at?"

"When I talked to Trixie, she said that she and Rocco were playing Russian roulette and doing Tequila shooters while they were screwing. "

"Yeah I know that; what's your point?" he said testily.

Kind of slowly I said, "What you don't know is there was someone else in the room videotaping the whole thing."

"What!" he exclaimed. "When were you going to tell me this little tidbit Finn?"

"Just chill dude," I said. "Do you want me to tell you what I think happened here or not?"

"Listen asshole, you have been withholding information that could be vital to this investigation and unless you start talking, I will personally take you in for obstructing justice as just the start."

~ ~ ~

"Look OJ, I was under contract as an investigator for Trixie's attorney and had an obligation to . . . . " I paused, "You know what? Fuck you. Figure it out yourself." I turned and began to walk away looking for Crutch. I was more than ready to head back to the house and Stacy.

To my surprise the usually hot-headed OJ said, "Wait Finn." He took a deep breath. "Let's hear it."

I stopped and let him twist in the wind for a full thirty seconds before turning back in his direction.

"If you look down to where the floor used to be, you will see what is left of a pattern showing that the blast spread down and out from this point here." I pointed to a spot on the floor in the center of three spikes of metal driven into the charred plywood.

"I think that the explosion began above this point. My initial call is that the explosive was on a tripod, most likely in a video camera, above this point. If we look carefully, we may find the remains of the camera and chemical residue from the explosive on it."

OJ seemed to think for a minute then asked, "So what do you think happened?"

"Well in the absence of a lot more analysis, I think what may have happened is someone, call him the unknown subject or unsub knew about the filming and wanted to get any witnesses out of the way. If Trixie had come home after she was released she would probably open the camera to take out the tape and boom she would have been taken out not the tape."

"Go on," he said,

"Well given that Trixie was already dead in the club, the unsub only had the person working the video camera to deal with. He sends the camera operator in to get the tape and as luck would have it, we show up while he is collecting it. The camera guy opens the camera with us outside and boom, last witness vaporized."

"OK, Finn, it's a nice theory but we have no proof. So now what?"

I thought for a minute and proposed, "Why don't you get one of your geeks in IT to do a search online for snuff porn. I'd offer to do it but Stacy is visiting and she already thinks I'm an over sexed pervert as it is."

"She's gotten to know you well, Finn. What are we looking for?"

"Given the video that was being shot, I wonder if the killing was accidental or intentional. Suppose they set it up for him to die. It may not have been the first one and there could be others out there."

"OK what are you going to do?" he asked.

"I doubt if the other girls at the club are going to talk to you but they might to me. I want to see if any of them have been asked to do films and see what I can learn. I'll just tell them I am following up for Trixie's lawyer to make sure she is treated fairly."

~ ~ ~

I headed back to the house with Crutch to see Stacy. As we drove down Truman I pulled in to an Adult Film Emporium. Crutch looked at me and curled up by the scooter. He probably realized there was no such thing as doggy porn and figured his odds were better on the street.

The plain grey wooden building had a large parking lot next to it with one or two cars in the lot. The ten by three foot faded billboard across the storefront was discrete and alliterative: *Bobby's Bodacious Booty Boutique*. In smaller letters, beneath the name as if the purpose of the place needed further clarification, was written *Cinema for the Discriminating Dick, Pussy or Asshole*. This counts for discrete in Key West.

A pimply kid with a neck tattoo of what looked like the head of a large erect penis sticking up above his wife beater slouched behind the counter. He was probably paid in free porn but on the other hand with the internet these days Bobby's was probably suffering and only catered to Luddites.

"Is Bobby around?" I asked.

"Who wants to know, asshole?" the kid smirked. Clearly this one had the makings of an intellectual giant.

"Fuck you, dick-head," I said with a smile as I walked toward the back where I assumed Bobby had an office. The kid came out from behind the counter with a leather sap in his hand. A sap is usually filled with lead shot and covered in tough leather so I assumed he was intending to stop me from interrupting Bobby.

"You can't go back there," he said swinging the strap hitting his palm with a loud THWAP.

I ignored him and continued walking down the aisle.

"I'm warning you. I'm not afraid to use this," he growled.

One of the things I learned on the force is people who need to threaten usually are reluctant to actually engage in a confrontation. *I was wrong.*

He swung the sap at my head as I turned to enter a door next to the aisle I had just walked down. I knew that a hit from one of these could knock you senseless.

I had been monitoring his progress in the big convex mirror in the corner of the store. It is positioned to keep an eye on homeless guys who try to crouch by the magazine rack for a quick jerk off without buying the magazine.

As he swung, I ducked and shot out a foot to his crotch. To my surprise I did not connect with the package I assumed would be there but rather a metal plate of some kind. He grinned and wound up for another swing. Now with a bruised foot I stepped back out of range to regroup.

This guy had now surprised me twice.

As he came at me again he feinted to my right, then tried a backhand swing. I deflected it up and to my left and drove a left upper cut to his midsection, then my right elbow connected with his nose. He went down like a bag of cement and lay still.

I turned to see Bobby shaking his head looking at his fallen security guard. "You just can't get good help these days. Finn, let me know if you're ever looking for a few extra bucks on the weekend or nights." He grinned. "Come on back to the office and tell me what's worth this amount of effort where a phone call would have been fine."

Bobby and I knew each other from my days with the KW Police Force when I had to bust him a couple of times for selling porn featuring underage girls. He knew I wasn't on the force anymore but clearly didn't seem to hold a grudge.

We caught up on local gossip for a couple of minutes

then I asked, "Bobby, rumor has it that somebody in town is shooting low grade videos featuring guns, meth and hookers. Have you seen or heard anything that raises that flag for you." I watched him carefully for any sign of knowledge and either he was a great liar or he had no clue about it.

"It's news to me Finn," he said with not a flinch or a twitch.

"Bobby I know you are tapped into the production of adult films in L.A. and Vegas. Have you heard anything about a new player doing things including snuff films?" He seemed to cringe and shrink in his seat. "What do you know Bobby?" I asked.

He reached into his desk drawer and pulled out a fifth of Jose Cuervo and reached for two glasses behind his desk. He poured a shot for each of us and tossed his back.

"Finn," he began. "We have known each other for over ten years. You know I have two daughters and have been married to the same women for over twenty-five years."

"Your point?" I asked.

"Look you may not like my business but I pay my taxes and employ at least two or three otherwise unemployable people in town. I paid for my girls to go to college and I even donate to Saint Paul's."

"Bobby, I know, I know, and you pay into the disabled pole dancers fund and the STD clinic for diseased hookers," I said with significant sarcasm. "What's your point?"

He reached into his desk drawer again and put a brown manila envelope on the desk. I let it lie there not sure what he expected.

"Finn, I found this inside the door of the store just this morning."

Chapter Eight

I REACHED ACROSS the desk and picked up the envelope on the edges to avoid leaving prints and pulled back the flap to shake out the contents. A single sheet of paper fell out. On it was a printed picture and a short note. It read in block letters:

"I BET YOU AIN'T SEEN NOTHIN LIK DIS BFORE SPECIALLY WHEN SHE PULLS THE TRIGGER. YOU CAN HAVE IT FOR $10,000. I'LL BE IN TOUCH."

There was a grainy picture of a man on his back with a naked girl straddling him holding a gun to his head. She had a shot glass to her lips and was clearly fucking him. He was smiling.

I looked up at Bobby and could see from his expression that this was something that even for him was beyond the pale.

"Have you ever seen anything like this before Bobby?" I asked.

He paused, then said, "Finn in my business you see a lot of things but this stuff is really hard core. It's hinted at on the *Silk Road* but I've never seen it. I always assumed that snuff films were an urban myth."

"What the hell is the *Silk Road?*" I asked having heard the name before but not looked closely into it.

"*Silk Road* is a site on the *Dark Web*," he explained. "It's usually used by drug traffickers using *Bitcoin* to pay for stuff but it's also a place to go for truly hardcore snuff and child porn, the white slave trade and murder for hire."

"Jesus Bobby. This is really sick."

"Finn you know me well enough that I would never push this kind of stuff but it's out there. You know from your days on the force that kiddie porn and child prostitution appeals to a certain *clientele* but we only sell the run of the mill teenage boy stuff like *Big, Bigger and Busty* or *Beastie Babes* or . . . . "

"Never mind," I interrupted him. "Wait, *Beastie Babes?* What the hell is that? Never mind, I don't what to know. Who do you think dropped this note off, if you had to guess?" I asked.

"Finn, it could be anyone. I don't have a clue but this kind of stuff is usually found online, not delivered in person so this feels more amateurish," Bobby conjectured.

"But hey, you're the detective. I planned on calling the cops today but wanted to see if this was just a prank before I had cops crawling around my store. You came in when I was still thinking about it, which is weird timing."

I thought about that for a minute and realized that he would not have heard about the film being shot with Trixie and Rocco so would not have made the connection.

"Bobby, let me call my old partner Jeff Sessions and have him come over discretely. He is a detective now and may want to set up a sting on this deal."

Bobby thought about it for a second then said, "Better yet, let's call him but meet him over at the Boathouse for happy hour. I usually go there anyway so it will not seem strange in case the store is being watched."

I called OJ and gave him a little color then suggested the Boathouse in an hour. I left the store with a copy of 'Naked *Surfer Muff Divers* under my arm. After all, I had to make the stop look natural so I couldn't leave the store empty handed.

Crutch and I rode the rest of the way home thinking about this new twist.

74

Stacy met me at the door with a kiss and looking down at the bag I brought in said in her best Mae West impersonation, "What'd ya bring me big boy?"

Shit, I was hoping she would be having a nap.

"Uh, it's a surprise," I improvised.

"Let's see it," she said excitedly grabbing the bag from my hand after a brief tug of war. She pulled the magazine from the bag and her eyes narrowed.

"What?" she retorted. "This morning wasn't enough for you? Now you are looking for a little *singular pleasure*?"

"It's not what it looks like," I stammered. "Well it is what it looks like, but it's for a case."

"What is it you're investigating? Surfer Moms you'd like to blow? Boy that is a surprise."

"No, no, sit down and I'll explain," I pleaded.

At this point Crutch had ducked into the bedroom but peered out from under the bed staying out of the line of fire but still taking in the fireworks.

It took about ten minutes but Stacy finally calmed down enough to hear the story and while she still seemed a little skeptical at least she wasn't looking ready to walk out the door. Crutch came back into the living room now that peace appeared to be restored.

"Coward," I quipped at him.

I took a quick shower to get the stink of smoke from the burned out trailer off me and changed into formal wear for Key West; white linen pants and a salmon colored linen pull over shirt with flip flops and my best Panama hat.

"I know you have doubts about my choice of reading material but let me make it up to you with dinner at A&B Lobster. I can meet you at seven tonight after I meet with OJ and Bobby for happy hour at the Boathouse."

I figured dinner at A&B would be a good call. After all, how can she be jealous of forty-somethings in a magazine? Clearly I had forgotten since my divorce three years ago that men never really understand women.

"I am still pissed," she muttered.

"We could skip dinner I could bring Chinese back here with a couple more magazines; maybe a current issue of *Silver Haired Studs* or *Wrinkles and Curlers?*

Daggers reappeared in her eyes.

Damn, too soon?

Then she laughed. "Dinner is fine but bring back a copy of *Silver Haired Studs* anyway. I'll see you at seven." And with that she headed for the shower. I fed Crutch, took a sneak peek into the bathroom and headed out to meet OJ and Bobby.

~ ~ ~

Another one of my favorite Key West Harbor hangouts, the Boathouse, is located on the edge of the old shrimp fleet harbor. Historic Marker number 77 is located at the epicenter of the Key West shrimp fleet. Florida pink shrimp were discovered off the Dry Tortugas in 1947. The new industry attracted nearly five hundred shrimp trawlers and thousands of fishermen and shrimpers. There could be so many boats in port at one time that it was said you could walk from one side of the Seaport to the other without ever touching water.

Fish markets, packing factories, icehouses, a cannery, brothels and rough bars followed. The bustling shrimp industry became a significant driving force in the local economy for two decades. The shrimping era is often referred to as *the pink gold rush.*

I looked up at the statue of Henry "Boots" Singleton, one of the first fishermen to capitalize on the shrimping industry, as I walked passed him in the harbor. It's good to live in a place that values its past although the local shrimp business dwindled long ago due to overseas competition and ever-rising diesel prices.

~ ~ ~

The Boathouse is one of the best places in town for Peel-and-Eat Shrimp even today and at half price during happy hour, one of my favorite watering holes.

I got a table by calling ahead to my old buddy Colonel Dave who could usually be found next door at the White Tarpon. For the price of a Dark and Stormy, his favorite drink, he wandered over to claim a table for us, then departed once I arrived. Bobby came in about ten minutes late and finally OJ looking like the cop that he is rushed in wearing his thick rubber soled shoes and his Salvation Army thrift store suit with a mustard stain on the lapel.

"Looking natty as usual, dude," I offered as he sat down. "Fuck off Finn," he rejoined.

I shifted gears. "We could keep this witty repartee going all day but we are leaving Bobby out."

"OJ, I would like you to meet Bobby who is a local entrepreneur . . ."

OJ interrupted me. "I know who he is Finn. He's a local sleaz-epreneur." He paused, "Offense intended," directed at Bobby.

"None taken OJ," Bobby offered showing a bit of style I thought.

I called over Melissa, my favorite server and we ordered a pitcher of Stella. After it was delivered, I asked her to leave us alone for a few minutes.

OJ, at Bobby's suggestion, I asked you here to discuss a recent case I have been working on. Bobby has come into possession of a piece of information that will require your assistance but could also benefit a recent case you have been working on." I paused for his reaction.

He seemed noncommittal so I thought it best to take the plunge. I looked around to make sure no one was in earshot and I asked Bobby to slide over the envelope he got at the store that morning.

"I was following a hunch this afternoon after I left you,"

I said to OJ. "I stopped at Bobby's store and thought it would be possible that Bobby might know where a certain type of video might be made and by whom." OJ was now listening intently.

"After a brief interaction with a worker, I went to Bobby's office to talk." I left out the details of the kid with the leather billy club.

Did I just say interaction? Perhaps I should have said altercation. "Bobby showed me this envelope after which upon inspection I realized you might have an interest and we arranged this confidential meeting."

I looked around again and passed OJ the envelope. Before touching it he asked, "Who has handled this so far?"

Bobby, not wanting to be left out jumped in. "Kyle the guy who opened the store today found it pushed under the door. I opened it and then Finn, but he only touched it at the edges and used a pencil to open it up."

OJ looked over at me and I nodded in agreement. He took the envelope by its edges and tapped the single sheet out onto the bar table on top of a cloth napkin. Taking a pen he opened it up and to his credit did not show any surprise. He slowly read the note and looked carefully at the picture that I assumed was a still shot taken from the video.

"We really get the intellectual giants here in Key West don't we?" he began. "So what do you propose?" he asked me.

"Well, this is your turf dude," I demurred, "but I was thinking perhaps setting up a sting to try and locate this rocket scientist," not wanting to give away any of our case info with Bobby at the table.

OJ seemed to think about this idea then asked Bobby, "Have you ever received anything like this before?" to which Bobby replied, "I get stuff stuck under the door all the time but it's mostly ad flyers, Christian End Times pamphlets, pitches for money or hate mail. I've never gotten this kind of *porn mail."*

OJ after a moment spoke, "Let me talk to our SMUT Team and see what they might know."

I had to ask.

"SMUT Team? We have a SMUT Team in Key West? If I'd known that, I might have stayed on the force. Sounds like the perfect assignment for me. What does it stand for? Sucking and Muffing Undercover Tactics? *I was pretty pleased with myself how quickly I came up with that one.* Do we have a PERV Patrol as well? Prick . . .

OJ cut me off and rolled his eyes at me. "Clearly we waited until you resigned before creating it." He hesitated a minute. "Finn, what are you looking for from me?"

"Ok here is the plan." I began making it up on the fly. "Bobby posts a big sign in the window of the store offering a ten thousand dollar prize for the best amateur porn film. Our objective is for the wacko who shot this video to submit it to claim the prize."

Bobby and OJ both starred at me like I was nuts.

Finally OJ said, "You're kidding right? Do you really think this guy is dumb enough to do that? His face was contorted like he had just developed a tic. "OK, I take that back."

Bobby was more thoughtful. "That is a great idea. I bet we will get some great videos."

Once a sleaz-epreneur, always a sleaz-epreneur.

"These are going to be evidence," OJ jumped in. "Not new products for your store."

Bobby looked disappointed but I think he liked the idea for the long term. I couldn't resist playing up the whole American Idol theme. I shared my vision of *Key West Porn Idol*, a sort of Girls Gone Wild porn meets Ryan Seacrest and Simon Cowell. I couldn't decide if I would be the witty charming one or the obnoxious jerk. I settled on Ryan.

OJ said he would run it by SMUT and get back to us the

next day. I offered to be a judge for the show and we broke up our little *business plan on a cocktail napkin* sting planning session.

~ ~ ~

With the next step in place, I rode home stopping at China Garden for some Kung Pao Chicken, Shrimp Fried Rice and Hot and Sour Soup. With food in hand and a bottle of Meiomi Pinot from Fausto's, I looked forward to a quiet evening with Stacy.

Little did I know the shit storm that was about to break over me.

~ ~ ~

Stacy put the Chinese food in the oven while I mixed a couple of my world renowned frozen concoctions. The martini glasses came out of the freezer and I dipped half the rim of each glass in Cream of Coconut then dipped that edge in raw brown sugar. Then I mixed two shots of vodka and a half ounce of Blue Curacao, shaken and poured in each glass.

The pale icy blue concoction with brown sugar around half the rim looks like a blue Tahitian lagoon. I call it 'Sex on the Beach'. With the wine opened to breathe, we settled on the sofa, clinked our glasses, took a sip from the blue lagoon drink and I brought Stacy up to speed.

"Let me get this straight," she said after about ten minutes of listening. "You are going to create *Key West Porn Idol* to smoke out a guy who shot a snuff film and you're going to be Ryan Seacrest to review this *pornucopia of smut*? Did I miss anything?"

"OK so when you describe it like that, it does sound a little crazy," I admitted.

Still not sure about her reaction, she smiled. "Can I be Paula?"

I laughed and realized she never ceased to amaze me.

We finished with Sex on the Beach then we finished our drinks. *Kidding.*

After I served up the Chinese food and Stacy poured the wine, we went out to sit on the deck to eat and listen to the piano player James at La Te Da. It was a mild evening and the breeze blew softly in the palms creating a quiet rustling that was a perfect union with the smooth sounds of the music in the distance.

I took Crutch out for a final fluid adjustment and he seemed to be restless and irritable. "What has got you in a mood?" I asked, as if he would answer. He seemed to be pulling me off our usual route so I let him lead. We walked back to Duval and instead of turning down Catherine he kept going until we reached the *Mockingbird* where he stopped short.

The place was locked up but as I peered in the window between the brown sheets of construction paper, I could see that our contractor Rico had made progress. The bar seemed to be finished except for the mirror behind it and half the bar stools, tables and chairs were unpacked and stacked in a corner. With the opening less than a week away I began to think we might actually make it.

I took out my cell phone and called Abacus. The phone went to voice mail after four rings so I said, "I just stopped by the bar and it looks like you've made real progress. Way to go. Sorry I have been a bit busy the last few days but I am looking forward to seeing you tomorrow. Let me know what I can do to help. Have a great night."

I had to yank on Crutch's leash, practically dragging him back toward the house for about a half a block then stopped. Something just didn't feel right. I turned back toward the bar and took a step when a muffled explosion shook the entire block.

Chapter Nine

I RUSHED BACK TO THE BAR and could see smoke wafting out of the saloon door to the kitchen. I yanked my keys off my arm where I carry them on a spiral elastic holder and jammed one in the lock. Rushing in and toward the kitchen, I stepped behind the bar and stumbled over a body face down on the floor. Flames had begun to show behind the saloon door and smoke was billowing out from the kitchen. I grabbed the body by its feet and began dragging him out to the street.

Sirens begin to howl outside and patrons from the Rum Bar, Grand Vin and La Te Da stumbled out into the sidewalks. A couple of burly guys from what appeared to be a wedding party based on their matching *Brian's Last Night as a Virgin* wife beater t-shirts rushed over and helped pull the body clear of the doorway so I could check if anybody else was in the building. I didn't make it far since a second explosion, probably gas, blew me back and flames licked around the edges of the bar lighting the new window treatments.

Damn, I had only just started to think of them as window treatments instead of shades.

The heat was building as I stepped into the room and suddenly the windows began to shatter out of their frames sending glass flying onto the street. I had to back out of the building again as the hair on my arms began to be singed by the heat.

The fire trucks arrived and with a rush of hoses and calm precision began to get the crowds under control and pour water on to the flames. The man that I had pulled from behind the bar was now on a stretcher with an oxygen mask on his face as an EMT was checking his pupils. He still seemed to be unconscious.

I yelled over to the fireman nearest me and said, "This is my place and my partner may still be in there." I took a breath and paused, it was only then that I suddenly realized why I had turned back. When I called Abacus's phone I could hear at the very edge of my hearing his ring tone, the steel guitar opening from 'Tequila Sunrise' from the Eagles 'Desperado' album. He had it turned up full blast but it didn't register with me until I headed back to the house.

The EMT had stopped working on the victim so I rushed over to see how things were going. I recognized the EMT as an old friend from my KWPD days.

"Steve, how's he doing?"

Steve replied in his thick Irish accent, "T'was touch and go thar for a wee bit. The vic's breathing was ragged and hay's got a nasty bump on the head but it could ha'e be'n a lot worse if he had been inside a that," pointing to the flames now pouring out of the front of the building.

When they pulled the mask off his face I confirmed for the first time that the man on the stretcher was indeed Abacus.

"Wee be tak'en 'im to Lower Keys Medical for observation and to make sure hay does nay ha've a concussion." said Steve as they lifted the gurney into the ambulance.

I stood on the sidewalk and watched the smoke and flames destroy three months of work and a hundred thousand dollars of my meager savings as the ambulance siren began its urgent journey to Stock Island and the Medical Center.

A hand slipped into mine and Stacy looked up at my stricken face saying, "We can start to clean up at first light. For now, let's go home and figure out how to get these bastards," as she handed me Crutch's leash. *This case had become personal.*

~ ~ ~

I woke up the next morning to a pounding both on my door and between my ears. Stacy and I had stayed up until two a.m. trying to sort out the pieces of the case. By the third Dark and Stormy, I had changed gears and shared with her my BUD/S drop and the pain of that experience.

Only four of the eighty members of my section from boot camp who went to BUD/S finished the program. It is still the toughest military training in the world and to quit felt at the time like my heart had been torn out. The loss of the bar brought back all the emotions of that day when I *rang out* as it is called when you leave the program.

Battered, injured, bleeding from numerous open infected abrasions, I concluded at the time that I was a drag on my boat crew. In SEAL teams, members rely on each other under extreme pressure and in lethal situations. I was a weak link so pulled myself out. On one hand I have selfishly regretted it ever since but my injuries took months to heal. I concluded that my body was not built to recover while those who completed the program seem to be able to heal quickly.

As Stacy and I drank and talked that evening and into the early hours of the morning, I came to recognize the stages of grief that lay ahead for me: denial; anger; bargaining; depression and finally acceptance of the situation. My past experience prepared me for the beginning of what I have come to believe is the cycle of grief not the stages. I decided to settle on anger, hang on to that one and leverage it to find the assholes who hurt Abacus and who were going to pay for the rebuilding of the Mockingbird.

I nudged Stacy with my foot hoping she would get up and answer the door but she barely stirred. I slipped out of bed and stumbled into the living room then to the door.

Pulling aside the blinds, I peered out to find Matt Divine my old BUD/S instructor glaring at me. I opened the door.

He barged in, took one look at the half empty Sailor Jerry rum bottle and said, "You look like shit Pilar. Put on some coffee and let's get to work."

"Wha the hell r you doin her?" I mumbled incoherently.

"Are you an idiot? he barked. "I had a call at five thirty this morning from the company you are insured with and they asked me to personally come down here and find out who blew up your bar."

I paused for a minute to collect my slow thoughts. "How the hell did they know about it?" I asked gradually coming alive.

"While you were getting drunk last night and feeling sorry for yourself, it seems your partner Abacus was awake at the hospital and called them to report the fire. They called me."

"I wasn't feeling sorry for myself . . . OK, I was. Abacus is OK?" I asked.

"Yeah, he has a nasty bump on his head and can't remember shit but when I talked to him as I drove down here he seems fine. Now get the coffee on."

At that moment, Stacy came out of the bedroom looking, disheveled, bleary and fantastic. She saw Matt and came over to give him a big hug.

"Matt, you are a sight!" she said excitedly.

He held her at arm's length and raising one eyebrow countered, "So are you!"

She blushed and replied, "Screw you and the horse you rode in on," turned and headed into the bathroom. "Glad you're here, Divine. He was getting a bit maudlin last night," and she closed the door.

I turned back to the kitchen and busied myself making a couple of double espressos and got out the eggs. "Have you eaten yet?" I asked.

"Yeah, I had lunch at Hog Fish on Stock on the way down," he said as he threw me a bag. "I brought you your usual."

~ ~ ~

Hog Fish Bar and Grill on Stock Island is my go-to place for a Hog Fish sandwich and I try to make it at least once a week. "Did you make it a double fish?" I asked. "Duh, is the pope from Argentina?" he responded. Old friendships are like fine wine; they get better with age.

I bit into the sandwich after cutting off a third for Stacy. I can be a bit of a selfish pig but I have come to appreciate her eating habits which tells me something is happening between us.

Matt finished his first espresso and slowly savored the second. "So where do we start?" he asked.

As Stacy showered I began speaking slowly.

"Four days ago, Stacy called me about a client Trixie who you may remember from the last case we worked on." He nodded and motioned with his hand for me to get on with it. "She was having sex, and drinking Tequila shooters with a guy Rocco Ramon. They were also snorting meth and playing Russian roulette."

"Jesus!" Matt exclaimed.

"Yeah, Darwin right?" He nodded in agreement.

"Needless to say it didn't end well. Rocco blew his brains out and Trixie pulled the trigger so she was charged. Stacy knew Trixie from high school so Stacy asked me to help with the case. When Trixie got released for lack of evidence the next day, I picked her up and took her to get her stuff at *Pussy Galore*."

"What. She's a stripper?" he asked.

"She preferred to be thought of as a *dance performer* and it's *was* a stripper," I corrected him.

"*Was*?" he inquired.

"I dropped her off in the parking lot of the club and

87

waited outside. She went in and about two minutes later she was blown into a fine red mist in the changing room."

The pupils of Matt's eyes dilated slightly but that was the only sign of surprise. He has seen a lot in his time.

"I ran into the club where smoke was pouring out of the back. Someone had rigged a grenade to explode when she opened her locker. At least that is what it looked like to me. To make a long story short, as a place to start, I was trying to track down the source of the meth when I ran into our old buddy Squeaky who you may recall tried to kill me working on the Linebush case."

Matt nodded again and waved his hand again for me to continue.

"It turns out Trixie and Rocco were stars of a video being shot - pun intended - when the gun went off. We think Squeaky was possibly the cameraman. It seems he went back to the scene of the crime to retrieve the video and got blown up for his trouble."

At this point Matt handed me his espresso cup for a refill and as I went over to make it, I continued. "It turns out the video is a snuff film that's now being marketed to adult video stores. I'm working with OJ who you know, to put together a sting to catch whoever is behind it."

I brought Matt's coffee over then said, "I think whoever is behind this film and now the three bombings are the same person."

"Wait a second, three bombings?" asked Matt.

"Yea Squeaky got blown up the next day in the trailer where they shot the video." I clarified, "Hence the assumption."

"That may be a safe assumption," he replited. "But let's not get ahead of ourselves. They appear to be connected but it could be that someone just wants us to think that."

I paused then said, "I hadn't thought of that. That's why you're the investigator and I am just the lowly sidekick.

Where do we go from here?"

"Well you're the EOD specialist and I'm not really known in town. How about you look into the bombings and I will handle the video part," he suggested.

"OK, then you will need to meet Bobby over at Bobby's Bodacious Booty Boutique," I said.

"You're kidding right?" he chuckled.

"I know it's island urban alliteration but it seems to work for him. He is the one who got a hand written note offering to sell him the video of Rocco's brains being blown out. We put together the sting and you will have to force yourself to watch the entries in the first ever *Key West Porn Idol* competition."

"You really are sickos," Matt laughed out loud then asked, "Alright as long as Stacy plays Paula, and I can play Simon but who will play Randy?"

"You haven't met Bobby yet, have you? He was born and raised in Bahama Village, dude. His family goes back generations after coming over from the Bahamas as ships' carpenters. Many of the original conch cottages here were built by them," I said giving him a little history lesson.

"I will tell him you're coming up to the store. You can take a look at the note and work on plans for the competition. It's going to take a week or two to get the videos submitted so you can come back here once you iron out the details."

I sent Bobby an email and gave Matt directions to the store. After he left, I thought I would hop in the shower then go over to the Mockingbird to assess the damage. Then Stacy came out of the shower wearing that damn kimono and thoughts of looking at our burnout bar disappeared.

"Where did Matt go?" she asked.

"He headed over to Bobby's to explore the porn side of the case. I offered to help but he said he preferred to look at porn alone. He's following his little head on this case I suppose but he said if he needed a hand he would call you."

She laughed at my bad pun and her robe slipped open.

89

Speaking of little heads. I reached for her and she said, "Slow down big boy. You need a shower after last night, then we can talk," as she pushed me toward the bathroom.

Before heading to the shower, I decided to feed Crutch who had been patiently sitting by the bowl while Stacy and I teased each other. The look on his face said, "Put it away dude and feed me."

I took the world's fastest shower and came strolling out all clean, fresh and upstanding, only to find Stacy dressed and heading out the door to walk Crutch.

"I hate to be a Debbie downer," she purred, looking down at my waist. "I can tell by the look on your . . . . , that you miss me. I'll walk Crutch and meet you at the Mockingbird. Now get that thing dressed."

Crutch seemed eager to go and pulled her out the door. "Thanks for your support, Lassie," I called after him. He looked back at me and bared his teeth. He hates it when I call him Lassie.

Before heading over to the Mockingbird I called Rico, our contractor, to meet me at the bar. "Oh Senor Finn, I am so very sorry to hear about the Mockingbird. I will meet you there," he said. And he seemed eager to get started on the cleanup but he hadn't even heard my plans yet.

Next I called the hospital to see how Abacus was doing and to talk to him if he was fit to talk.

"Lower Keys Medical Center. How can I help you?" a young voice answered.

"Could I speak to Abacus Finch please? He is a patient who was admitted last night."

"One moment please," and I was on hold.

After about six hours, well more like a minute, but it always seems like six hours, Abacus answered. "What?" he growled.

"Well I can tell by your cheery greeting you are recovering," I offered.

"Finn, get me the fuck out of here! These people are nuts!" he howled. "They've been poking, prodding and putting things up my ass. It's worse than Guantanamo Bay under Bush."

I laughed out loud.

"It's not funny man. They have me sleep deprived after a night in the same room with a homeless guy with the DTs and the food is, well, you know how I feel about Jell-O." He took a quick breath. "Get me the hell out of here!"

"Ok, I am going to stop at the Mockingbird to meet Rico then I will be up to get you." I offered.

"No, I need to get out now man. For all that is holy, get me out of here."

Now you have to know that Abacus is a committed atheist so for him to invoke the name of God was a sign of desperation.

"Alright, I will be there in fifteen minutes," and as I hung up I heard him scream, "Make it ten!"

I called Rico and told him I would be picking up Abacus then meet him in about half an hour.

I threw on some clothes and as I rushed out the door Stacy was walking Crutch back to the house. I grabbed his leash, kissed her, stopped, kissed her again, paused for a quick fantasy then ran for my scooter. Damn she is a good kisser. "I'm going to pick up Abacus," I shouted and we hopped on the scooter.

We made it to the hospital in thirteen minutes to see Abacus waving his arms to get my attention and dodging an orderly trying to get him to sign some paperwork for his release. He hopped on the scooter and said, "Step on it. They want me to sign a credit card slip for my treatment and it's already maxed out from the Mockingbird."

We sped down the drive with the orderly chasing us on foot waving a sheaf of papers.

Chapter Ten

ONCE OVER COW KEY CHANNEL and back on the island, we cruised down Flagler and I dropped the speed to a roaring twenty-five MPH.

I updated Abacus over the sound of the wind as we drove. "We are meeting Rico at the Mockingbird to assess the damage and develop a plan. I have an idea and once we see what the damage is and talk to him about the work required, we will be able to tell if it is workable."

Abacus seemed a little woozy as we rode but we made it to Duval and parked in front of the *Bird*. We decided to shorten the name and call it the Bird because it reflected what we had lost. The sign out front was half burned and all that was left was 'bird'.

Rico was waiting out front and was on his cell phone as we parked.

"Senor Abacus, you are OK, yes?" Rico asked as Abacus climbed gingerly off the scooter.

"Eighty percent, Rico," he countered. "Working on ninety once we see the shape of the bar."

The three of us walked in through the damaged door and it looked like the place was a write-off, at least to me. As we wandered through the bar area and into the kitchen, it went from bad to worse. The floors were water damaged from the fire fighting and the walls were scorched and the ceilings falling in. The tables and chairs were damaged and the bar was half burned out. The kitchen was a complete mess with fire and water damage everywhere.

"OK," said Abacus, "Make it sixty percent. This place is a mess."

"No, No Senors," said Rico. "I can make it ready in *dos*

weeks, at least to open."

We both looked at him like he had been doing tequila shots all morning or at least smoking something.

"No really. Clean up will take two days and the tables and chairs we had not unpacked in the back did not get burned or wet. The biggest issue is replacing the windows and making sure that there is no structural damage." Rico's accent had suddenly disappeared. "I have already called my structural guy and the clean-up crew to get started plus I have talked to my window guy and he can have the hurricane windows ready to go in ten days once I give him the go ahead."

Abacus and I were speechless.

We unpacked a table and four chairs and I decided to share my idea. When we arrived at the Bird and saw the damage I was ready to discard it but thanks to Rico I thought it might work.

"OK guys, here is the plan."

After ten minutes they both sat in stunned silence.

I called Matt and Stacy to join us. Once they arrived I went over it again with them. They smiled and we got to work.

~ ~ ~

Key West's biggest and busiest event on the island is Fantasy Fest. This multi week event takes place at the end of October each year and includes numerous parties, parades, body paining, drag queen contests and debauchery. I used to have to patrol as a cop; now I just go to ogle breasts and turn a blind eye to the old guys who really should cover up.

During the final week, there can be upwards of fifty thousand visitors thus tripling the island's population. Since it was scheduled for three weeks from now, leveraging it fit perfectly with my plan.

~ ~ ~

I spent the next twenty four hours, going over the Bird with a fine tooth comb to figure out how the fire started. We began working with Manny Rodriguez, the Key West fire investigations specialist. Who knew Key West now had one of those? In the end we concluded that the fire was started in the kitchen using one of the oldest tricks in the book.

Ironically, the accelerant used was a couple of bottles of our own hundred and fifty proof Sierra Silver Tequila. Our bar was planning on specializing in tequila tastings with over two hundred different offerings.

Whoever set the fire simply disconnected the gas line behind the stove, poured a couple of bottles of the hundred and fifty proof tequila on the kitchen floor and into the bar. He lit one of the table candles and placed it on the kitchen floor and then walked out the back door. The flame from the candle appeared to have ignited the tequila, then that ignited the gas that then exploded.

With most of the kitchen destroyed there were no fingerprints to find. Because Abacus was knocked out at some point and left in the bar, it was not just an arson case but attempted murder. If I hadn't come in when I did, he would have been toast. Extra crispy.

While I worked on getting the fire investigation completed, Stacy worked on permits for the repairs, Matt worked with Bobby and OJ on our sting and Rico began coordinating the clean-up and reconstruction. Crutch, well, Crutch ate, peed and slept.

We agreed to get together for happy hour at Spencer's by the Sea in the Reach Hotel to add some variety to our diet.

At five, we met in the bar to compare notes. Richard, the Jamaican bartender took our orders and while we waited for our martinis, nachos and burgers, each of us did a rundown of the day. You can't do a rundown without fuel. Crutch tried to impress Richard with his latest trick, the back flip, and he actually stuck the landing. Richard added a slider to the order for Crutch forcing me to eat my whole burger without his help.

Matt started us off. "I worked out the details with Bobby to place an ad in the Citizen tomorrow announcing the *Porn Idol* competition to be held at the Grand Opening of the new Mockingbird Tequila Bar – home of the soon to be world renowned Tequila Fireball."

Matt was really getting into this.

"The first Porn Idol star would be selected the day before the Fantasy Fest parade. The ten thousand dollar prize money should stir up some interest. The copy would read: Each film is limited to three minutes and must be an amateur production. They must be submitted with contact information, names of the actors and a release that the films can be used for promotional purposes. Entries are due in two weeks."

"So how can we be sure the people who sent Bobby the snuff film will enter the competition because they won't use that film, will they?" I asked.

"They need to let us know how they want to get paid and the point of the competition is to show we are interested in the video," Matt explained. "I expect they will submit a video with something that lets us know they are the maker of the 'Trixie video."

"OK" I said, "but let's think of other tracks we can come up with to find these guys in case this one fails. On another issue Matt, have you got approval for the insurance claim so we can pay for all the stuff we need to do?" I asked.

"Not yet but you know what these guys are like. Given my track record with them I know they will pay but we just don't know when. Be prepared to self-fund for the next thirty days or so," Matt advised.

Sounding a little desperate I replied, "I can't self-fund for the next three days much less thirty days. Rico what can you do for us?" I inquired.

He looked a bit pensive and said slipping back into his Hispanic accent, "Oh, Senor, I am but a poor man with many mouths to feed and I need to pay my workers Friday each week. I can cover you for maybe a week but will need cash for supplies and the windows." He shook his head and seemed to regret his decision to get involved in this extensive project.

"OK, look. I have a guy who has been asking to make an investment. Let me talk to him and see what I can do. How much do you need?"

Rico paused for a calculating minute then said, "fifty thousand should get us to the end of the month if I stretch it."

Damn I thought. I'm in the wrong business.

"OK, you will have it," I promised.

He seemed relieved. "You are the best my friend." Yeah, me and a thousand Uncle Benjamins. *Am I being too cynical?*

"Stacy, where are we with the permits?"

Stacy looked down at her notes and walked through a list of required permits and progress on each. Key West is a beautiful place to live but the building codes and permitting process are a nightmare.

Our food arrived and my appetite had been decidedly dampened by the perfect ice-cold martini straight up with two olives and the nachos, a massive and divine pile of chips, cheese, chorizo and chilies. As we all tucked in and drank, the nightmare of the last forty-eight hours seemed to fade, at least for a sunset. Even Crutch relaxed and took more than one bite to eat his slider.

After dinner I shared my conclusions about the fire and my next steps. I did not share my plan to shake the bushes as a backup in the event that Porn Idol didn't produce more than ten or fifteen three-minute teasers for teen age boys or horny old retirees.

~ ~ ~

Something Trixie had done when I dropped her off at the club triggered a thought for me. She said she was going to collect some clothes and her last paycheck. I recalled a recent article in the paper about a suit by some of the girls at another club for back pay or minimum wage and the clubs saying they were not paid by the club as an employee, but rather they rented time on the floor and collected tips.

If she was not going to pick up a paycheck, then what?

And she had more bounce in her step than Monica when she got home with her stained blue dress.

What gets a meth addict stripper that energized? It's probably not the latest issue of HGTV Magazine. She had been in jail for more than twenty-four hours and was probably on a meth crash. I needed to talk to the other girls to see what they could tell me.

~ ~ ~

I told Stacy I was going to Pussy Galore and would be home as soon as I could.

Not really . . . .

I told her I had a lead I needed to check out and would get it done and be home before ten. She is an understanding person, but I would rather have something to report than just deal with suspicions. *Or so I told myself anyway . . . .*

I dropped Stacy and Crutch off at the house. Crutch has never been a fan of strip clubs; too much Patchouli on his sensitive little nose I guess so I left him behind.

I motored along Simonton to Eaton and up to the club. At eight thirty it was just beginning to come alive.

Nothing had changed since my last visit and no I don't mean as a customer. There was a new door on the changing room and a girl was up on the stage dancing to a Prince song with purple lights highlighting her enhanced money-makers and a sequined thong. Several other girls were standing by the bar sipping rum and cokes and watching for potentials for a lap dance.

I waved an attractive brunette with a flimsy cover up over to my table, ordered a drink and offered to buy her one as well. She brought over the drink - coke with a splash of rum - and sat on my knee. I know what you are thinking, tough duty right? Well you try and have a beautiful half naked girl sit on your knee and ask a coherent line of questions while she rubs your thigh. If we had used this approach at Guantanamo, we would have been out of Afghanistan in a year.

Natalie – I would be willing to bet her real name was Natasha – was incredibly beautiful with a charming, but barely understandable eastern European accent. Between sips of my diluted drink and her stroking my thigh it took me a couple of minutes to get around to asking the first question.

The image of settling in for a long night of *questioning* crossed my mind but hey, I was on duty and had a deadline.

"Natalie, what is a beautiful girl like you doing in a place like this?" I'll bet she has never heard that one before.

She smiled patiently pretending it was the first time she had been asked that question and replied after a thoughtful pause. "I am loving America and for me this is way to be here. Home is not good place for me. Father and brothers drink too much and look at me strangely."

I dutifully bought this line having heard various iterations a dozen times from strippers when I was a cop. I sometimes think these clubs have an orientation program for strippers before they get started. It didn't matter if they were from Russia, the Ukraine or Arkansas; it was always the same.

"I am so sorry you had to run away from that. How did you end up here in Key West?" I replied with just the right amount of empathy and encouragement.

"I have friend who helped me get into America with student visa and I am taking English classes at college here." She smiled and rubbed my thigh again.

I could feel myself stirring and figured I better move this along.

"Good for you," I offered. "That's how to get ahead in America." Wrong choice of words but she didn't seem to notice. They clearly hadn't covered puns in her English class yet.

"I had a friend who worked here. Her name was Trixie. Did you know her?"

Natalie suddenly looked both sad and a little frightened. For the first time, it appeared she had a genuine reaction to me.

"Trixie not here anymore," she said as she stopped rubbing my thigh.

"Really?" I acted surprised. "She seemed to be very happy here when I saw her several months ago. What happened?"

"She not here anymore," Natalie repeated while standing up. "You want another drink? Maybe I dance for you?"

Well, in for a penny, in for a pound as the saying goes, which these days means at least a fifty. I nodded.

She took my hand, waved to the bartender/bouncer and walked me over to a corner and into a private room. I paid her fifty bucks and she waited for the music to start for the next song on stage while taking off my shirt. She began to move seductively while moving closer to me swaying to and fro to the rhythm of the music and inviting me to take off her top. I reached up and took her shoulders and gently pushed her away.

During my Navy days I had been through a program called SERE or Survive, Evade, Resist and Escape. It included being put through several enhanced interrogation sessions. I am going to recommend resisting and escaping Natalie's obvious charms to my old instructor Matt Divine as a final test. Few would pass but luckily I am older and wiser so will fight it.

"Natalie, you're a beautiful girl and please keep dancing but tell me what happened to Trixie."

She missed a beat but continued and said, "Can't talk about it. They will hurt me," as she kept dancing.

"Who are *they*?" I could barely get it out as she shook her head and leaned forward slipping off her top and rubbing her soft breasts against my chest.

She whispered in my ear, "Cameras in room," then she pulled back, turned and began to sway her seductive, finely formed ass toward my lap. Thankfully it was covered by a thong. Perhaps covered is the wrong choice of words; *highlighted* might be a more apt description.

I imagined some guy in a little room somewhere watching us as Natalie did her thing and I pretended to be aroused or pretended to pretend to be aroused. Did I say she was a beautiful girl with a perfect ass and . . . You get the picture? Thankfully I didn't have to stand up as the music began to wind down.

I flashed back to high school math class with Cathy Roberts sitting beside me as I imagined us under the bleachers. The teacher interrupted my adolescent fantasies.

"Pilar, quit daydreaming and write the answer to the last question on the board." I could barely stand much less answer the question and had to use a textbook like a fig leaf to hide my stiffy.

Natalie leaned over and brought me back to reality. "You want more dance?"

"No not now," I offered suggestively, "but maybe we can meet after you get off for a more private session."

"Is not allowed," she replied.

She turned and taking my hand walked me back to the

main room then she climbed up on stage to do her routine.

I sat and watched for a few minutes then walked over to the bar where other girls were standing. Selecting a rather thin blond with a couple of obvious enhancements, I asked her to bring me a drink. I was beginning to appreciate the watered down drinks they served and when she came over to my table my routine began again.

After the third girl answering the same questions, the same way I came to four conclusions: All the girls were eastern European; they all had the same father/brothers; and were all students studying English with greater or lesser success. Finally, they were all afraid of some unnamed *they* but none would talk to me about Trixie.

I left after two hours and almost four hundred dollars poorer. The drinks, while watered down, still cost me almost twenty-five bucks each with tip.

OK, so I did have a few more lap dances.

My third partner was Petra from the Czech Republic and she got me for three dances. *It was late and I was on my sixth coke and rum.*

Chapter Eleven

I KNEW STACY would be waiting up at home and after two hours in the club I knew I would stink of smoke, booze and cheap perfume - not the best combination - to show up at home wearing.

I looked at the scooter and figured the drinks were weak so I was probably good if I took the back streets. OK, I was not thinking as clearly as I might have otherwise. I *almost* made it. Lights started flashing behind me. I heard a disembodied voice over the megaphone.

Now you have to be driving badly in KW to get pulled over. One guy I know on a scooter was stopped at a red light and forgot to put his feet down. The scooter toppled over and he looked up from the ground at a drunk, homeless guy leaning over him in the middle of the street asking if he was OK. After picking up the scooter and brushing himself off the homeless guy asked him for twenty bucks.

I pulled over to the side, stopped and waited. The car pulled up behind me and a familiar voice said, "Finn, you idiot, you know better. Shut it off and I'll give you a lift home. Also we need to catch up."

As I climbed into the back of the police car, OJ said, "Jesus man, you need a shower. You smell like a cheap hooker after a night giving blow jobs behind a perfume counter." Then of course he laughed at his own joke.

I politely chuckled, as I was the one in the back of the patrol car, then told him, "Fuck off, I've spent the last two hours undercover at Pussy Galore trying to get a break in this case. I've been forced to drink bad booze and watch strippers perform up close and personal. You try that some time. No. Wait. You do that all the time."

We both laughed and then as he drove me back to my place I gave him an update. "I'm not sure how this will play out but all of the girls except the deceased Trixie are from Eastern Europe. They all have student visas to study English and they are all terrified to talk about Trixie because *they* won't like it and will hurt them if the girls talk."

"So who do you think are the mysterious *they*?" he asked.

"That's the million dollar question. Trixie said when I picked her up, that the club is busy over lunch till about two, then the girls take a break and go somewhere to sleep then the evening shift starts at five thirty. I am going to see if Stacy can go over to the club tomorrow and follow them home to see where they live. I have an idea to at least track down who *they* are."

"Just be careful," OJ said. "In case you haven't noticed, your friends have been targets lately. If they connect you and Stacy . . . " On that somber note he dropped me off and I slowly walked up the side of the house.

Stacy lay curled up asleep on the sofa on the back deck. The fire pit was still putting out a bit of heat and the mosquito zapper was doing its usual crackle every few seconds killing the random bugs not wiped out by the Mosquito Control Board helicopter dropping its chemical load every few weeks.

She stirred when I sat down next to her and her first words were, "Go take a shower, you smell like a cheap hooker after a night on the street."

I began to wonder how so many people knew what cheap hookers smelled like. OJ I could figure out. I guess Stacy being a lawyer had probably come across a few cheap hookers the day after they were arrested and she helped them after they posted bail.

She appeared to fall back asleep so I took advantage of

her suggestion and hopped in the shower. When I came out she was asleep but this time in my bed. Probably just as well after my six cokes and rum.

~ ~ ~

I awoke to the smell of fresh coffee and bacon. Stacy was wearing one of my old Tommy Bahama shirts and that appeared to be it. She smiled when she saw I was awake and offered coffee which I gratefully accepted.

"Morning sleepy head," she teased, "Rough night last night?"

"You don't want to know," I said hoping we could move on to a different subject.

"Oh, but I do," she replied with a bit of an edge to her voice.

I filled her in on *most* of the evening leaving out my occasional woody and only shared a general description of the girls.

"Sounds like you had a *hard* night," she quipped.

I chose to ignore the pun and replied, "Actually, it was quite a productive evening and I have an idea, if you are up for it."

"Depends on what you mean by, up for it," she replied sarcastically.

Clearly I was not yet on firm ground so I thought a bit of a breather would help.

"Let's eat and we can talk about it over eggs," I offered.

With that I cooked the scrambled eggs with some spinach and gruyere, then plated the bacon and a half an English muffin for each of us and we headed for the back deck.

"Let me share the idea and you can tell me what you think."

"Oh-oh-kay," she said skeptically.

"Alright. Trixie said the girls at Pussy Galore take a break after the lunch crowd leaves and go home for a couple of hours rest before the after work crowd arrives around five thirty. I will go with you and we can sit down the street from the back of the club, wait for them to leave, then follow them home." I paused and she seemed to be following along.

"Once you know who we are targeting, you can approach one of your choosing and see if you can get her to open up."

"How am I going to do that?" she asked, clearly not sure what she would do.

"Here is the tough part. You could say you're looking for work and had been a dancer in college for parties. You could . . . ."

"Finn, are you suggesting I get a job at Pussy Galore?"

"No, no, no," I stammered. "Just pretend to be interested in order to find out who helped them get in."

To my surprise she said, "Well, I guess we are going to have to see if I am qualified first."

She stood up, went into the living room, and turned on the Bose. Strains of *You Can Leave Your Hat On* by Joe Cocker began echoing from the room and a hand was slowly revealed through the door holding one of my Panama Hats.

Unhurriedly, she stepped through the doorway wearing a thong and a cutoff t-shirt. She began to move to the beat of the song and I forgot about everything but her body and the music.

By the end of the song she collapsed naked but for the hat on the sofa and said breathlessly, "What do you think, do I get the job?"

I was speechless.

She smiled looking down, "Based on your reaction, I think you must have missed out on a happy ending last night." She took my hand and led me to the bedroom. "Why don't we take care of that?" she said as I followed her seductive little ass.

Gotta love this girl.

106

By the time I awoke for the second time, it was almost noon. I apparently needed my beauty sleep. Stacy was in the living room online with her phone to her ear talking with the city working on building permits and inspections dates for getting ready for the big opening.

After a quick shower, I called Matt to see what progress he had made with the insurance company if any.

"I talked to my contact at the company and he is going to see if he can walk it through the system for me but he wasn't optimistic. The bureaucracy in these companies is crazy," Matt said. "The good news is the paper agreed to publish the Porn Idol ad in today's paper and we got a prime space on page two above the fold and the entertainment editor wants to do an interview with Bobby who I proposed as our host, Ryan See-crust. It seemed like a fitting name for a porn host."

I laughed and it just seemed to encourage him to really get creative.

"I'm still working on the guest judges. What do you think of J Lo No-Lower, Steven Tie-her, and Semen Cowlick?" I laughed so hard Stacy said, "Will you boys keep it down. I'm trying to sound professional to the city."

I signed off with Matt and fixed Stacy and I some lunch while she waited on the phone to get the legal side of our project on the right footing. Once she got off the phone, we talked about the plan for the afternoon.

"I will point out the girls I talked to last night once they come out of the club, then we can follow them home. They said that they came to the U.S. on student visas and were taking English courses at the college." She nodded so I continued, "See if you can find out who was the person who recruited them, brought them here, and got them their visas and jobs."

"How am I supposed to do that, Finn?" she asked reasonably.

I paused and offered, "How about telling them you have a half-sister in Montreal who would like to come down to the U.S. but she was arrested last year for solicitation and needs to come here on the QT. You can just say, oot and aboot and throw in a few ehs and they'll buy it."

She looked at me skeptically and said, "Never mind, I'll think of something, but thanks."

I knew she would be as good on her feet as she was in the sack.

We kicked around a couple more ideas and then headed out with Crutch on the floorboard. As we rode up Eaton I turned a block before we got to the club and we parked. Two people walking a dog, even a three-legged one is not really noticeable and it gave us some plausible cover as we walked toward the back of the club. It turned out there was a small coffee shop with a couple of benches across the street from the back of the club so we ordered coffee and chatted waiting for the girl's shift to end.

"Here comes Natalie," I said, and she walked right passed us without a pause.

Stacy looked at her and said, "You didn't tell me they were cute." She glared at me.

"Did I fail to mention it?" I replied trying to look like a choirboy after a fart in church. "Here come two more. I saw them at the club but I don't know them."

Stacy stood up and as they came into earshot, she slapped me, and shouted, "One coffee and you think I am going to fuck you? Screw you asshole! I don't need your crummy job that badly." She began walking quickly after Natalie who had turned down Caroline toward Duval.

Stacy got to the corner and looked both ways as if not knowing which way to go, then leaned against a stop sign and started to cry.

No matter what you think of strippers and their stereotypes, these two were not heartless. As they walked by me they swore under their breath something unintelligible but probably asshole in Russian or Polish. As they came up to Stacy, they appeared to offer her help and Stacy began to walk along with them.

I watched them turn onto William Street and enter what appeared to be a large pink Victorian gingerbread house with a set of stairs going up the side. It seemed to be a typical Old Town rooming house with a high-end vacation rental on the main floor and two or three apartments in the upper floors.

I couldn't very well hang around out front and wait for her so I headed to the Southernmost Café for an early happy hour Bloody Mary. I had missed my exercise routine for the last couple of days so thought a Bloody Mary would at least maintain my reputation with Cindy, another one of my favorite bartenders in Key West.

As Crutch and I rode down Duval, I noticed Abacus out in front of the Mockingbird, directing Rico as he hauled a set of burnt cupboards out to a dumpster on the street beside the bar. Clearly they had been at it for a while because the dumpster was almost full of damaged chairs, tables, curtains, and bar fixtures. A Service Master truck was out front with hoses and big disk cleaners to scrub the floors.

We pulled over to check out progress. I spent the next hour with them both working to get the demolition and clean up complete. As we finished getting the kitchen cleaned up my phone rang. It was Stacy.

"Finn, you owe me big time for this one," she began, "These girls are in deep shit and we need to help. You're not going to believe who's involved. Can you pick me up at Schooner's in ten minutes?"

I was out the door in a shot with Crutch at my heels.

Chapter Twelve

STACY WAS STANDING out in front of the bar waiting for me as we pulled up and she invited me inside. "I need a drink," she said as I parked and we found a table by the water and ordered a couple of Dark and Stormys for us and a Bud Lite for Crutch. I waved to Miguel, my favorite cigar guy who has a stall in the bar, and he sent over three of my personal Robustos.

When the drinks arrived she began, "As you probably guessed, I rejected the sister in Montreal idea and waited until you pointed out a couple of girls you didn't know. I figured I would throw you under the bus as the sleaze employer and work the sympathy angle. In case you are wondering, you are trying to get me to turn tricks in return for a place to stay with you. You are a bad guy in their mind. It seemed only fair after your little evening's *entertainment* last night."

I am not sure I agreed but I understood.

"You are not going to believe where this went after a few tears and a couple vodka and tonics. The girls took me up to the room they share with, get this, four other girls from the club. It seems that they are all from the same town in Slovenia and were recruited to come to the U.S. by a guy named Georgi. Sound familiar?"

"Holy shit, Sherlock!" I exclaimed. "How can that be? Is it the same guy? He's in jail."

"Wait, it gets even better. It turns out these girls were brought over on student visas with the promise of free education, and jobs in the *entertainment* business. Georgi lends them the money to pay for all their travel and visas. He holds their passports and takes eighty percent of the tips they earn dancing so they can pay for renting time on stage at the club and for the apartment. They have to pay the loan back before they get their passports returned. That was nine months ago. Once they're here a year, they are threatened with deportation because the student visa runs out and then the real fun begins."

Stacy continued breathlessly, "Based on what I pieced together from other girls who have been here longer, he then gets them involved in making videos. First it is just one of them dancing but soon it involves soft-core porn, girl on girl, simulated sex and oral sex. Finally, some of the girls have gotten into drugs that he makes available and they start doing real hard-core stuff: orgies; unprotected sex; animals; even snuff films. They are scared because about three months ago, Georgi stopped coming around and a new guy took over. Drum roll please. A guy named Eddie."

You could have knocked me over with a feather. "Not our old Eddie?" I asked.

"The very same."

"Jesus."

In my last case, Eddie Ransom, my long time financial advisor, turned out to be the gay lover of my ex-wife's second husband. It's a long story.

Georgi was a Russian Spetsnaz Special Forces Operator who I had helped put in jail for attempted murder. *Of me.* Georgi was the bodyguard for a long time Key West family whose patriarch was the father of my second wife's gay husband. It's a really long story.

I ordered another round of Dark and Stormys for us. I must admit this case was becoming even more compelling.

"So what you are telling me is Eddie has picked up the pieces and is now running this human trafficking scam while Georgi is in jail?"

Stacy nodded then added, "This is not a small problem. Most people think of sex trafficking as a problem in some third world country but it is huge in the U.S. It has been estimated by immigration officials that as many as ten thousand women are being held in underground brothels in Los Angeles alone and Florida is one of the top three U.S. destinations for sex trafficking."

As I shook my head slowly, she continued. "It is estimated that you can buy a woman for ten thousand dollars and get your investment back in a week."

I was at a loss for words at the numbers.

"It looks like we've stumbled onto somebody's personal ATM and it's no wonder they're going to such lengths to protect it. We need to get you back to my place." I paid the bill and with a nod to Miguel for the cigars, we headed out the door of the bar with Crutch at our heels.

Back at the house, I called OJ and Matt who both showed up in about thirty minutes. It's a small island.

"Guys," I began. "Stacy just got us a break in the case but we only have hearsay and no evidence. Stacy why don't you lay out what you found."

Stacy told them her story and heard plenty of, "No shits and sons of a bitches," as she walked them through it and they were brought up to speed.

OJ, ever the cop asked, "Will they testify to all this?"

Stacy replied, "It's still just hearsay. We need to prove that Eddie is running these girls and he is smart enough to shepherd them as simple students making a few bucks working the club and they are paying for rent. Even though it is very expensive rent, nobody is really breaking the law - at least not yet."

I thought about this for a moment then offered, "I wonder if Trixie was involved in this deal but was just further along in the cycle. If she came here more than a year ago, then perhaps her student visa was up and they began threatening her with deportation and at the same time getting her into meth and the porn stuff. I haven't seen her in at least four months." I paused.

Damn, could I have triggered her being killed?

I continued, "I first met Trixie when I was trying to find a drug dealer to pressure during my last case. I actually met with him in the morning before I picked her up. It was Squeaky. Squeaky was blown up as well and if Billy is a part of this, then he may have given Eddie a heads up that I was looking into this case."

As the wheels were really turning now, I yelled out, "We need to find Billy, NOW!" If Eddie is covering his tracks, then Billy could be next."

OJ was on his feet and on his cell phone.

"Hillary, it's Jeff Sessions. Can you please put out an all points on Billy Conroy, five foot eight, a hundred and fifty pounds, brown hair, picture in the file? Wanted for questioning in the bombing of Pussy Galore."

My jaw dropped as I realized that OJ knew Billy; although in hindsight, I'm not sure why I was so surprised. Billy was a known sleaze.

I figured the best place to find Billy was at his favorite haunt so I decided to go over to the Green Parrot. I headed for the door and Stacy started to follow. I turned to face her squarely.

"If Billy is a target then clearly so am I, so you should stay here with Matt," I said firmly to Stacy.

She started to protest but OJ said, "Finn's right, you need to stay here."

"Screw you two over-protective misanthropes. I need to be with Finn to keep him out of trouble. He's liable to be a bit - how shall I put this - overzealous in his interrogation of Billy when he finds him."

She was right of course. I had had about enough of these perverts.

"All right, but Crutch, you need to stay here."

I needed to assert my authority with someone.

He looked at me with such a forlorn scowl that I consented, "Ok you can come too." *Next time I will be firm.*

I asked Matt to cover Abacus at the bar and the rest of us headed out.

~ ~ ~

The Green Parrot is only about three minutes from my place if you get the lights right and tourists don't wander out on the road not paying attention to lights or stop signs. We were there in less than that. Crutch figured it was a beer run and seemed disappointed that we didn't immediately order a round. I think he may be developing a taste for Bud Light.

As I scanned the bar, I could not see Billy at his usual spot. Tonight was Sound Check. It is the session the bar hosts for locals on Friday and Sunday night's beginning at six. Billy was almost always in attendance. I did not like the fact he was not there. Where the hell was he?

We stood at the bar for a few minutes listening to the band and waiting to see if Billy showed up. Suddenly I could hear a siren in the distance. Slowly the sound built and soon it seemed to drown out the band as it tore by the Parrot headed up Whitehead. This is a common enough occurrence on the island between tourists with heat stroke and drunks after three or four too many but I had a bad feeling about this one.

Chapter Thirteen

STACY AND I WALKED OUT onto Whitehead with a few other patrons in time to see the EMTs pull up about two blocks away near Eaton. A small crowd of tourists was gathered near the corner. A scooter lay in the road and people seemed to be milling around by the curb watching the EMTs working on someone. A downed scooter is usually a tourist riding one for the first time showing off to a girlfriend with a few too many under his belt.

We walked down the street as the rest of the folks and Crutch went back into the Parrot as the band started to play their next song.

As we came to the corner, it was clear that the person on the scooter was not in good shape. Lying in the intersection he did not seem to be responding to the efforts of the EMTs.

Close to the scene I noticed a husky sunburned woman in a tank top and a pair of velour short shorts with the word Juicy emblazoned across her ample backside. *They really shouldn't make that brand in that size.*

I asked what had happened and she said, "Some idiot in a big SUV ran the stop sign, cut off a car, rammed into the scooter, stopped, looked at him then took off. It was almost like they meant to hit him."

With a sinking feeling I looked past her and toward the person on the ground. The EMT's efforts had become less frantic and they seemed to have stopped working on the inert body on the ground. I walked across the street to get a better look at the body but I knew even before confirming it, that it was Billy. Whoever was behind this had just cleared up another loose end.

OJ pulled up and came over to the corner on which we stood. "The call just came in from the EMTs that the victim is deceased. The ID is Billy Conroy."

I nodded knowingly.

"Witnesses said a light colored SUV appeared to intentionally run the stop sign and hit his scooter, pause for a second, then took off. As usual people were so shocked they didn't get a plate number or see the driver. We set up a roadblock at Cow Key Bridge but my bet is the vehicle is stolen from the garage of a snowbird who lives north of the Mason Dixon line. The driver then just returns the SUV back to the same garage. We won't find it until the snowbird comes back to Key West in two or three months and notices his vehicle is damaged."

The accident investigation team had begun to block off the area so Stacy and I headed back to the house picking up Crutch on the way.

Crutch preferred to stay at the Parrot on his favorite bar stool watching the band and didn't join us for the walk down to the crash site. I suspect car crashes reminded him of the one when he lost his leg. Some drunk tourist on a Harley cut a corner, jumped the curb and hit his previous owner killing him and crushing his puppy's leg. I got him from the shelter after his leg had been amputated and never did know his real name so the name of Crutch seemed perfect. We both were in need of some support at the time. He still cringes slightly whenever he hears an ambulance.

As we rode the scooter back to the house Stacy asked, "Now what?"

After a pause, I said, "Here is what we know. Girls are being brought here on student visas then coerced into first performing as strippers to pay back the money they borrowed to come here. We suspect that once the visas expire, they are forced little by little into drugs and pornography. Once they have begun to lose their looks as the drugs waste their bodies, they may be sold into turning tricks in underground brothels or worse they simply disappear. For all I know, it may have been that Trixie was supposed to put the gun to her own head and she screwed up and put the gun to Rocco's head instead."

As we discussed it further, an idea began to form. Rather than share it with Stacy, I called Matt. "You busy?" I asked.

"Only if you consider a man of my many talents busy when he is scraping burned and bubbled paint off the walls of your bar trying to get it ready for paint," he harped "Otherwise, no I'm not busy."

"OK, I have an idea and I need some back up. Can you meet me at Smokin' Tuna on Charles Street in fifteen minutes?"

"Got it."

Stacy was not happy when I told her to wait for me at the house and even less so when she saw me get my H&K USP .40 from its locked drawer. I covered the Blackhawk paddle holster with my Tommy Bahama shirt and began to leave.

"Be careful," she said then added, "Can I have Crutch if you shoot yourself?"

"He's yours."

~ ~ ~

I rode up Whitehead and parked on Caroline Street walking the rest of the way down the alley to Smokin' Tuna. Matt was already sitting at a table in the corner with a couple of beers.

"Actions, orders and ROE," was all he said.

As a former Navy SEAL, Matt although retired, is still the consummate professional. SEALs are meticulous when planning a mission and a work up can take days or even weeks depending on the complexity and risks. Actions, Orders and Rules of Engagement are basic to any plan.

Having said that, they are also accustomed to improvising. The old saying 'We plan; God laughs' is never truer than in battle. "Ruck up, find the bad guys and kill them if you must."

He stared at me.

"Just kidding," I chuckled, "But the look on your face was worth it."

"Here is the deal. There are four major Gentleman's Clubs in town, Pussy Galore you already know. They are actually all owned by the same guy, Rufus Hornet. He goes by the name Stinger."

Matt chuckled at the nickname.

I continued, "I know, I know. A bit cheesy, but I suspect it refers to his dick. Stinger runs several restaurants and bars as well as the clubs. He is rumored to make regular flights to the Caymans to deposit money in an off shore account. I ran across him when I was with the KWPD but while we suspected him of running a variety of scams, we could never prove anything. Stinger likes to throw his weight around which believe me is considerable both in pounds and influence."

Matt was taking all this in, simply nodding occasionally.

"Stinger keeps an office in the club which you may have noticed next door.

'The *Green Door*," Matt snickered.

"I know it's a bit old school but I think it was started in the '70's."

"All very interesting but what is your plan, Finn?"

"Patience, patience. I suspect he is the one behind the importing of these girls and Eddie is only a front man. Eddie was never an original thinker and last time, he was just following orders. He's also not a killer," I added.

"My plan is to confront Stinger, tell him Trixie put me on to him and I want a piece of the action. I expect he will deny it but who knows. He has never met you so you being my bodyguard should work. Your job is to make sure we both make it out of there."

"Not much of a plan," he remarked but said, "Let's go."

The Green Door true to its name was a glitzy club with a bright green entrance and a picture of Marilyn Chambers smiling down from a poster on the wall. I didn't imagine many of the current patrons even knew who she was. The after dinner crowd was fairly light and the girl on stage just appeared to be going through the motions although the motions were still pretty good. The sound system was pounding out *You Shook Me All Night Long* by AC/DC which seems to be part of a typical strip club sound track. I wondered if they all just buy the same mix from some teenager running a web site called *Strip Club Hotties* or *Shake your Booty.*

We walked up to the bar. I leaned in to be heard and said to the bartender, "Stinger around?" I got the usual reply. "Who wants to know?"

"Just tell him his mother called and wants me to come around again tonight." The bartender stared. "You are dead, motherfucker." and went to the phone in the corner of the bar.

Rufus came charging out of the back with some muscle head behind him then stopped when he saw me.

"Roofie baby," I said. I actually preferred that name for him as I know it pisses him off.

"Well if it isn't Officer DOR Pilar," he said, "No, now you are just DOR Pilar." He turned around and said to his muscled head, "Throw this quitter out of my bar."

Muscle head stepped forward to grab my arm and found himself on the floor with a broken wrist and an elbow at risk.

Now right-handed guys usually assume that most people are also right handed and grab for that hand to lock up the stronger arm. As a lefty, it is easy for me to reverse a grab, and pull the other person toward me. I can then push back the arm bending the elbow and lifting it up with my left putting pressure on the shoulder socket. I can twist the wrist forcing the guy down hard and breaking the wrist and often knocking them out.

I have never liked it when people called me DOR so I went ahead and broke the elbow and popped his shoulder for spite.

"Roofie, you need to get better help dude. You forget I did end up in EOD and KWPD. Now can we talk?"

Stinger looked around and saw no sign of help on the way so he asked, "Who's your lap dog?"

Matt replied, "I'm his proctologist. I told him I was looking for some new assholes and he brought me over to see you."

I broke up.

Stinger looked like he would take a swing at Matt.

Big mistake I suggested with a telepathic glance.

He thought better of it and just said, "What do you want, Pilar?"

"We should probably go to your office for a little privacy," I suggested.

He turned and we followed him as he waddled down a narrow corridor and into a large office in the back of the building with a private entrance leading to the alley in back. The office had a big flat screen TV with cameras focused on the stage and several private back rooms. It appeared that Stinger liked to watch his girls work.

His oversized office chair groaned as he sat down heavily. "So what the fuck do you want asshole?" he politely asked.

"Roofie, Roofie, Roofie," I began, "I just wanted to offer my condolences for your loss."

He stared back at me trying to process what I just said.

"What loss?" he asked.

"Roofie, how can you say that? I was told you and she were close."

"She who?" he asked again.

"Trixie of course."

The light began to dawn but he quickly went into denial mode.

"Trixie who?" he recovered.

"Come on Roofie, let's not dick around. You had Trixie as a dancer for over a year and she was last seen walking into Pussy Galore before she was blown to kingdom come, in case you missed it."

"Right, right Trixie. I forgot her name. Yes very sad, thanks for the sympathy but next time just send a card. Now leave," he demanded.

"Not just yet Roofie. You see I was the one who picked her up at the Monroe County Lock up and took her to the club. Before she died, she and I had a little chat."

"So?" he asked.

"So I decided to get myself a little cut of your action."

He laughed. "And what action is that?" he quipped.

I had decided to begin with the strippers shooting porn films, then ramp up to snuff films, then broach the whole sex trafficking thing.

"Trixie told me you are using the girls to shoot porn and then selling it online."

"Pilar, you are such a putz. Every stripper in the world wants to get into the movies so we shoot a few videos now and then. Get the fuck out of my office."

"Ok Roofie, I'll leave but then I will have to share what else she told me. . . . . about the murders."

"Pilar you are so full of shit. What murders?"

I could see that sweat stains had suddenly begun to show on his shirt.

"In the snuff films you're making."

"I have no idea what you are talking about," he said with a snicker but his nervous laugh was apparent and the sweating beginning to show on his collar.

"Are you getting nervous Roofie? You're sweating like a stuck pig."

"Get out Pilar before I call the cops on you for assaulting one of my staff."

"Here's the deal Roofie. You are going to pay me ten percent of the gross receipts of the clubs every week. Plus a one-time fee of one hundred thousand up front to cover my losses on the Mockingbird after you blew it up."

"WWWhat the fuck are you talking about? Are you saying I blew up your bar?"

"Just like you blew up the Pussy Galore and the trailer on Stock where you filmed the strippers," I replied.

"I had nothing to do with blowing up your place," he countered.

"So you *did* blow up your own place and the trailer."

"I didn't say that."

"No, but we call that in an interrogation, *truth by omission*."

"Get the fuck out Pilar. I am not going to pay you a dime."

"Ok Roofie, I think you should take some time to think this over before you decide. You have twenty four hours," and I turned to walk out.

"I don't need time to decide," he yelled.

"If you say so but then I am going to have to spend some quality time with Eddie," and I slammed the door behind me.

Now you may be judging me for throwing Eddie under the bus or in this case, Stinger, which amounts to the same thing, but Eddie was responsible for the importation of dozens of young girls into a life of degradation and shame. He was also at least partly responsible for the death of my ex-wife and her father.

Now we just needed to find Eddie and warn him that he was in Stinger's sights. *Kind of an apt metaphor if you ask me.*

As we walked out of the club I turned to Matt. "My proctologist?"

Matt chuckled and said, "I've been saving that one for a special occasion and it just seemed to fit."

~ ~ ~

As we rode back to the house together, I pondered what I had set in motion. When you poke a tiger, even pointing it in the direction of the prey, doesn't mean it will follow your instructions. It can just as easily turn on you for poking it.

One thing that troubled me about Stinger's comments was his denial that he had blown up the Mockingbird but did not deny the others which involved the murders of Trixie and Squeaky. I wondered if there was a copycat out there simply coming after me and hiding behind the crimes of another.

We pulled up to the house and after a hug from Stacy she punched me in the shoulder.

"Hey, what was that for?" although I probably could have guessed.

"You ungrateful asshole. I risk myself to get you the information on the sex trafficking and you left me out and didn't even tell me where you were going," she shouted.

I looked over at Matt and he shrugged as if to say, "Leave me out of it dude." Then I turned to Crutch who just covered his ears and closed his eyes. Cowards I thought; I was clearly on my own.

"Don't look to them for support. What happened?" she asked.

For the next ten minutes she grilled me like a prosecutor and I filled her in on most of the details trying to leave out the more sordid bits and in the end said, "Now do you see why I didn't tell you what we were doing? You would have first tried to talk me out of it and second been guilty of breaking about a dozen laws which as a lawyer you can't afford to do."

She seemed a bit contrite but still protested, "You could have at least told me where you were going in case you got into trouble."

I decided to concede the point, "You're right I should have had you as a backup." *Perhaps this would buy me some nooky.*

Mollified she asked, "What's our next move?"

"Well, I said. "We need to get some rest then tomorrow we need to find Eddie."

"I can help you there," she said. "He has a boat on Stock Island called, *The Covered Call* that he has been living on since he lost his broker's license."

"How do you know that?" I asked.

"Well, while you boys were our playing investigators, I went looking for Eddie."

"But I told you to stay here."

"Which I did but you can learn a lot on the internet. I remembered that Eddie used to work with you on your investment portfolio and he sold covered calls for you and also for Courtney."

"OK," I said. "So far so good."

"I searched the SEC records which I have access to through our law office in Tampa looking for old asset declarations from Eddie's time as broker. One of his assets was a thirty-two foot catamaran named *Covered Call*. With the name, a quick search of boat registrations in Florida showed he was registered at the Stock Island Marina. A call to the office there revealed that yes a Mr. Edward Ransom keeps a boat by that name on a mooring."

She ended with a, "Ta Da!" and lifted her arms for a round of applause.

"Damn girl, you are dangerous," Matt said. "If you ever need a job call me. You could be a great investigator."

She smiled and took a bow.

"OK," I replied. "Do we go there tonight or wait till morning?"

Now one thing you should know is that Navy SEALs love two things: working at night and preferably in the water.

Matt jumped in. "Look we have set Stinger on a path and we need to make sure that Eddie survives any attempt on his life. He is the guy we need as a witness. We need to go now!"

Chapter Fourteen

I GRABBED MY DIVE GEAR and the spare set I kept in a shed behind the house,threw it into the trunk of Matt's car then we headed up to Stock Island. I asked Stacy to track down Eddie's boat and text me the location as we drove to the marina.

"So what is your plan?" Matt asked as he drove.

"Working on it," I replied as I tried to figure out how Stinger would respond to what we had told him.

"Let me try this on you," I offered, "You tell me what you think."

"Assuming Stinger is the guy who has been using explosives to get rid of Trixie and Squeaky, then I think that might be his preferred method here as well."

Matt nodded so I continued, "He benefits by being able to have an alibi when the bomb goes off. I suspect he is going to place a device on the hull of the boat, probably on a timer, so he can be in a public place when it goes off."

Matt nodded in agreement then added, "I think your basic idea is correct but I have trouble seeing Stinger doing this himself. He weighs over three hundred and fifty pounds and is unlikely to do his own dirty work. Who do you know who is capable of setting explosives?"

"You mean besides you and I?" I asked.

Suddenly the face of Nikos Cross popped into my head. Nikos Cross was the father of my ex–wife's now deceased husband. His son Peter was the gay lover of Eddie Ransom. I know it sounds weird but they were a highly dysfunctional family - even more than most.

The Cross family was deeply involved in a variety of criminal activities in Key West but when the only son was killed by me and then the body was lost at sea, the old man seemed to go underground. In the past, old man Cross employed an ex-Spetsnaz contractor Georgi who ended up in jail for attempted murder, *of me.*

Spetsnaz is the Russian military counterpart of the Navy SEALs; highly trained, extremely capable, deadly Special Forces operators. Given the eastern European connection in this case, namely the girls brought in as strippers, could Cross be involved and have another Spetsnaz contractor involved?

"Matt, this may have just gotten a bit more complicated." I shared my theory with him as we pulled up near a ramp several hundred yards from the marina.

"So you think Stinger may be working with Cross?" he asked.

"Well think about it. Cross used to work with that wacko Georgi who almost killed me on several occasions before he got caught. What is to keep Cross from finding another guy like him?"

Matt ever the sensible one said, "Let's not jump to conclusions. So far the explosives have been pretty rudimentary. Having said that, let's keep an eye out for a more serious player than Stinger."

Once Stacy texted the location of the cat, we each put on our BCD's and air tanks. We checked each other to make sure everything was done up right then walked down the ramp toward the water. We then donned our fins and masks and began to swim out to the *Covered Call.*

Navy SEALs and EOD specialists spend hundreds of hours training and operating in the water at night. I had fallen in love with Key West while training here and after leaving the Navy and marrying Courtney, moved back. Let's just say I was happier in the water than I was with Courtney.

Matt and I swam on the surface toward the mooring to which we thought the *Covered Call* was attached. About one

Lewis C. Haskell

hundred yards from the boat, we submerged to about twenty feet and continued swimming toward it. As a rudder came into view above us, we slowly rose together at the stern to just under the swim platform on the starboard side hull.

Lifting my mask I was able to confirm that this was the right boat and that someone was on board moving around on the back deck. We swam between the two hulls and I whispered the outline of my plan.

"You take the port side hull and I'll cover the starboard. Look for anything unusual and keep an eye out for another diver. If it's all clear, I will go onboard to talk to Eddie and you cover us from under the boat."

We both dove down about five feet and began inspecting our respective hulls. After another full five minutes of careful inspection, Matt gave me the OK sign and I swam to the stern of the starboard hull and gingerly took off my fins. I inflated my BCD so it would float just at the surface. I pulled my H&K out of the water proof pouch on the BCD, hooked the spare regulator on the swim ladder and slowly climbed the boarding steps molded into the transom until I could peer directly into the cockpit.

Eddie was sitting on a padded lazarette with his back to me working on his laptop. My weight on the starboard boarding steps caused the boat to shift a bit and he had looked up. He turned to see me with my dive mask perched on my forehead and the gun pointed at his head. Must have scared the shit out of him and he froze.

"Hello Eddie," I said in a friendly voice. "Long time. Thought I would stop by to see if you had any option ideas for me," and I grinned but no comment from him. "We need to chat."

He started to get up so I said, "Sit!" as I waved the gun.

I slowly climbed the rest of the way up the boarding steps and stepped down onto the deck of the cockpit then sat on the seat by the wheel.

"So . . . Eddie . . . I think you have a serious problem," I began. "Your little tits and jiggles business is about to need a new supplier."

He paused, looked a little surprised then collected himself. "Get the fuck off my boat, asshole," he began.

I fired the .40 into the bulkhead by his head.

I had forgotten how loud this gun is. I must have awakened half the island, yet as I looked around I didn't see a single light come on or any apparent reaction in the marina.

"Jesus", he said. "What the fuck man?"

"Eddie, you need to understand, I'm not fucking around with you. Do you remember the last conversation we had involving you and a very nice Wolf Gas Range?" I smiled at that comment; this is a longer story but he knew what I meant and still had the burn marks on his butt to prove it. I enjoyed seeing him squirm in his seat.

"Now tell me about your little recruiting business with Stinger," I said pointing the gun up slightly.

"All right, but what has it got to do with you?"

"Just talk asshole," I said.

"After you caused me to lose my broker's license I was jammed up. The SEC was looking at me for fraud and the court took over my oversight of the Linebush estate. I lost my house and figured I would disappear for a bit and live on a boat. I needed to make a few bucks and I had been working this gig for a couple of years on the side."

"What gig is that asshole?" I asked wanting him to confirm my suspicions.

"The girls," he simply said.

"What girls?" Be specific."

"Look, I had a contact, in eastern Europe who was looking for a guy to work the U.S. side of an import business."

"Be specific Eddie."

"He wanted to help girls get into the U.S. I helped him get visas and then helped them get jobs. What's so bad about that?"

"Eddie, you are either a complete idiot or a complete asshole and I'm voting both."

Suddenly, our conversation was cut short.

The bullet didn't kill him but took a big chunk out of his scalp. By some accidental miracle, it must have clipped one of the stainless steel stanchions that supported the lifelines around the boat. *In his case, they really were lifelines.* He fell to the deck bleeding profusely from the head wound. An inch to the left and the bullet would have killed him. As it was, he was just knocked unconscious and would have a hell of a headache when he woke up.

I dove onto the deck after him as the next shot pounded into the side of the boat but still no sound.

I could hear the shots slamming into the side of the hull chewing up the fiberglass and the interior of the starboard hull and potentially working their way up to the cockpit coaming as we lay prone behind it. We needed to get off the boat but Eddie was dead weight.

I checked Eddie's pulse and it was still strong. His breathing was regular but I needed to stop the bleeding and we needed to get off the boat. I began to feel the starboard side settle slightly and realized that the bullets must have punctured the hull just below the water line. As water seeped in and the hull settled, the holes higher up the hull would begin to leak as well. In my experience, boats that fill with water usually sink. I didn't know if a cat could float with only one hull but didn't feel like putting it to the test.

I didn't know Matt's current location with respect to the boat and only prayed he didn't decide to come up on the starboard side to check out what was going on. I also had not been able to see where the shots were coming from. A

133

long-range rifle with a suppressor on it could be as much as a thousand yards away so my little pistol was useless at that range.

As I lay on top of Eddie - which is not a pleasant experience given what I know about his sexual orientation and his preference for wearing tutus during sex - I remembered a trip I once took on a catamaran.

During the owner's safety briefing, he pointed out an emergency hatch on the inner side of one of the hulls under the stairs to the cabin that could be used in the event that the boat flipped upside down in a storm. If this cat had such a hatch, I could drag Eddie down into the hull and out the hatch. I needed a distraction.

Even an experienced warrior, knowing that a pistol shot is out of range, has a tendency to flinch when they first see a muzzle flash at night. The H&K .40 is a powerful handgun but its maximum range is only about two hundred feet. Until you know what you are dealing with, you at least flinch when you see the flash.

I didn't want to risk hitting another boat if I just fired in the direction of shore. I decided to aim low at the water and in the general direction of shore. I figured whoever was hunting us had a night vision scope so the flash might also blind him for a second and let me get over the side.

I had given up the adrenaline rush of combat more than ten years ago and with a beautiful woman at home and a comfortable life on a tropical island, this was really not how I wanted to spend my time. Unless you are a real hero or a nut job, being on the wrong end of a sniper who clearly is an expert is not how you want to spend a tropical evening.

I pictured an ice-cold extra dry martini straight up with three blue cheese olives and a double plate of Dijon crusted lamb pops. I raised the .40 above the coaming and fired almost a full clip low and in the direction of shore, then dove over the stern of the cat.

I felt a round from the shore nick my calf as I entered the water. *Son of a bitch I am too old for this shit.*

I came up between the hulls and began to look for Matt. He surfaced next to me.

"Dude, I see you still know how to make friends," he quipped.

"It's my charming personality and big gun, I think . . ."

"So now what? And what's happening with Eddie?"

"So here's the deal. We need to get Eddie into the water and to shore. He was grazed by the first shot from whoever's on shore and he's unconscious. I need you to go onshore and try to drive the guy there off or at least distract him so I can swim Eddie to shore."

"No problem. He may or may not know I am with you so let's assume he does and that he knows our backgrounds. I will take your tank and swim with it up to and under the dock making sure he sees the bubbles. He will most likely think Eddie is dead and will be following the bubbles. You can get back on board and patch up Eddie."

"Then what?" I asked.

"I will raise the tank up in the BCD under the dock and give him a target. Once you see him hit the tank, I will release the air and sink it. Hopefully he will think he has killed you and pack up, but I will go after him either way. You go back to the car with Eddie and get him to Lower Keys Medical pronto. We need him alive."

"Sounds like a plan except for the part about him killing me."

We parted with a soggy fist bump and I swam over to the port side to look for the escape hatch. Toward the inside center of the hull was a small plexi-glass covered opening that appeared to be under the port side companionway. Small was a generous description but any porthole in a storm as they say.

I waited about five minutes after I watched Matt

unhook my tank and BCD off the stern swim ladder, then I dove under the port hull. I reached up and grabbed the port side rail to chin up onto the deck. In the SEALs we did this all the time but I realized I needed to hit the gym a bit more. I used to do fifteen dead hang pull-ups without breaking a sweat but too many Bloody Marys seemed to have had an impact on my muscle tone.

After struggling to get a leg up and hooked on a stanchion, I decided it was blood loss from the calf wound and not the Bloody Mary's. Denial is not just a river in Egypt. I lay winded on the deck hidden from view of shore. I then slid back to the cockpit and over the coaming. After peering toward the dock for several minutes, I saw a flash and the sound of a tank releasing air with a loud whoosh. The tank appeared to slowly sink with bubbles ascending to the surface and after a minute stopping. So far so good.

I love working with professionals.

I could almost feel the night vision scope swing back to the boats and I waited. Suddenly the night lit up with muzzle flashes as Matt opened up with his Glock firing toward the flash that *killed* me.

I grabbed Eddie by the back of his tattered shirt and dragged him down the companionway into the port hull. I was not particularly gentle which didn't seem to matter as he was still out cold. He was also the asshole who was trafficking young girls and forcing them into porn and prostitution. Whatever he got, he deserved as long as it didn't kill him. I needed him as a witness and as a threat to Stinger.

I hauled the companionway ladder out of its cradle and opened the porthole under the inside hull. I positioned Eddie so I could get out of the hull first then drag him after me. I could have pushed him out first but he might drown before I got out myself.

I must admit it did cross my mind.

136

Keeping the starboard hull between the shore and me, I used a lifeguard rescue hold to sidestroke slowly toward the ramp where we had left the car. As I came out of the water Matt came up beside me.

"Boo" he said.

"Nice work man," I said gratefully.

"No problemo dude" he replied adding, "Once I started firing I could see in the distance he headed into the mangroves. I expect he had a boat in there and took off. I didn't get a good look at him but he moved like a pro and his rifle had a big suppressor on it."

Suddenly, an explosion sent huge gouts of flame towering into the air in a fireball where *Covered Calls* had been moored. The blast wave even at two hundred and fifty yards almost knocked us over. Once we looked back toward the boat it was essentially just bits of fiberglass floating down onto the water.

"I guess the shooter made a quick stop before he took off. Probably wanted to make sure Eddie was dead," Matt surmised.

We dragged Eddie over to the car and after a bit of effort sat him up in the back seat. As we drove toward the hospital, Matt asked what I had learned from Eddie.

"He basically confirmed that he was helping get visas and jobs for the girls but he was shot before he could tell me who his contact was. As far as he was concerned he was just a middle man who was helping these girls get into the country."

"So what is our story when we bring him into the hospital?"

I thought about it for a minute as we pulled in to the emergency entrance of the medical center. "How's this?" I proposed. "We were driving by the marina and saw an explosion. We stopped and while looking out at it, saw this guy in the water. We dragged him onto shore but he clearly

137

needed medical attention so being good Samaritans we're bringing him in."

"I like it," Matt agreed. "The gunman actually did us a favor." Matt was always a half glass full kind of guy.

Chapter Fifteen

I CHECKED EDDIE'S POCKETS to make sure he had no ID on him then went inside. A gurney was brought out to take our *John Doe* into the ER. I spoke to the person at the admissions desk giving her our story. She made notes, took our names and we headed out.

As we drove back to the house, the night's activities began to catch up with me. My calf was still leaking blood even after the quick field dressing I applied in the car before going to the hospital. Matt was a *be prepared* kind of guy and kept a Field Medi-pack in the car.

Pretty much every muscle in my body ached as the adrenaline rush wore off. I needed a drink, a hot tub and a good night's sleep.

"Do you want to come in for a drink?" I asked Matt hoping he would say no.

"Sure," he chirped then he paused, "Just kidding. You look like shit dude and you need to get some . . . ." He paused again, "Sleep."

I laughed. "Do I look like I could do anything but sleep?"

He let it pass and dropped me off saying, "I will call OJ and let him know that Eddie is at Lower Keys Medical and may need protection. You get some rest."

I stumbled to the back of the house and inside to find Stacy curled up dozing on the sofa. I leaned over, kissed her and she stirred.

"Well hi there big guy," she said, slowly uncurling her legs.

"Hey beautiful. Buy a guy a drink?" I asked.

"What time is it?" she replied sleepily.

Checking the clock on the wall behind her I said, "About half passed dead by my body time."

"You look like shit, she said, parroting Matt's assessment of my condition. "Why don't you strip and rinse off while I make you a drink?" she offered.

"I like the drink and strip parts. Are you having fantasies about taking advantage of me in my weakened condition?" I asked.

"Only if you wash off the sweat and salt stink, then tell me what you were able to learn for all the obvious effort."

"OK, but make my martini a double and I'll be back before the olives hit the bottom of the glass."

After the shower, I changed the dressing on my calf and going commando with anticipation, I threw on a pair of clean khaki shorts.

Looking at the dressing when I came into the room she asked, "You want me to kiss that better for you?" as she brought over the drink and a glass of Pinot Gris from Oregon for herself.

"I can think of other things for you to kiss before that," I suggested.

"Talk first, fun later. Now sit."

Don't you love a woman who takes charge?

For the next ten minutes, I gave her an outline of what happened leaving out a few details and minimizing the wound to my leg. The reality was that for all the risks we had taken, I had confirmed at least part of my theory but was in reality no closer to finding out who was behind this scheme nor having any proof. Unless Eddie came to and was willing to talk further, then testify, we had nothing.

Stacy could see that I was beginning to fade so taking my hand she led me to the bedroom and slowly pulled my shorts off.

"Well, well, well" she said smiling. "I thought you were

half dead, but I now see which half isn't."

She slipped off her shorts and pulled her top over her head. Stacy is a beautiful, uninhibited woman and I must admit she was a sight to behold. "Is that a Brazilian?" I asked jokingly as I reached for her but she pushed me gently back on the bed, bent down and took me in her mouth. With a groan, I lay back. I decided she wasn't going to answer my question.

After about thirty seconds she stopped, and climbed on top of me.

Gently she began to kiss me on the neck, the chest and my belly as I lay savoring the attention. For the next thirty minutes she took charge. Luckily I am a *mature* guy, or it would have been thirty seconds.

Alternatively shifting positions on the king size bed, she would tease me to the edge, then allow me to return the favor. We explored each other's bodies, discovering new areas of sensitivity and excitement. *Calf injury? What calf injury?*

She gradually allowed me to take command and she began to moan as if I found new places to taste and caress. As her hips began to move to my touch, more and more urgently her back arched and with a cry and a shudder, she came and came again, each time with a soft cry. Gently I kissed her thighs and climbed up to her head kissing her as she lay panting softly.

I lay back enjoying the sensation of pleasing such a beautiful and sensual woman when she stirred, reached over and began to kiss me again taking me in her mouth. I reached down and slowly invited her to climb on to me. I entered her gently and we began to move in the age-old manner of the lover's dance.

She began to move more and more quickly and with a cry of, "Fuck me, Finn!" her back arched, her breasts thrust above my face and we came together eyes wide open and our 'O' faces on full display.

Slowly she lowered her body fully on to mine and we lay panting, then breathing more slowly together.

"For an old injured guy, you seem to have a lot of energy. Time for a rematch?" she asked smiling.

An old Toby Keith line came to mind, which I had to sing. "I'm not as good as I once was, but I'm as good once as I ever was." She laughed and we rolled apart.

I would like to say that after a sip of my martini and few minutes of sexual banter, we continued on for the next hour.

Truth be told, I awoke as the sun came up with the martini untouched and our legs entwined in sleep. I lay on my side watching her sleep and wondering how I had become so lucky.

She stirred and reached over for me with a smile.

"Hey sleepy head." I teased, "You fell asleep on me last night."

"You fuckered me out," she grinned, "but I have a feeling it was mutual."

As I caressed her breast feeling myself stir, a knock came at the door.

"Ignore it," she said, her voice husky with barely concealed lust.

I leaned over and kissed her when a knock came on the bedroom window behind the blinds.

"Hey kids. You can paw at each other later. We have work to do," ordered Matt.

"Fuck off Matt, but you could take Crutch for a walk," I yelled.

He chuckled and used the very inventive key-hiding place under the mat to come in and get Crutch. I limped out of the bedroom. Crutch looked pissed off at me for my ignoring him for so long but appeared grateful that Matt was taking him for a walk.

I fired up a pot of coffee, turned on the oven to preheat and took out a frozen Gordon Food's 'Bacon, Egg and Cheese casserole. As the oven hit four hundred, I threw in the casserole and called to Stacy, "Breakfast in ten minutes."

"Come back to bed!" she beckoned and I was sorely tempted but knew Matt would be back shortly.

Are you kidding? I ran to her in a mad dash as fast as a guy with a bum leg could go.

Stacy was standing fully clothed and laughing. "I wanted to see what you would do but we need to get moving."

The hangdog look of disappointment on my face must have been priceless because she laughed even harder then came over and kissed me.

"We'll have plenty of time for that later. I hate to rush a good thing. She smiled gently, "Now let's have some coffee and talk about what comes next."

Matt and Crutch came in as I was taking the casserole out of the oven and I doled out four portions; well three and a half. Crutch needed to watch his weight. We sat on the back deck and ate breakfast discussing next steps.

"We know that Eddie was doing fine until we talked to Stinger so it is a safe bet that he had something to do with the attack last night, agreed?" I offered to get the conversation going.

"While we can't be a hundred percent sure, I think it would be a big coincidence otherwise," Matt agreed.

"We also know that the shooter last night appeared to be a professional and military trained. He is also probably the guy who blew up the boat and is potentially the guy who killed Trixie, Squeaky and probably Billy in the scooter accident. Finally, he could be the one who set fire to the Mockingbird and tried to kill Abacus."

They all agreed.

"So who is this guy and who does he work for?" Stacy asked.

At this point I shared my thought about Nikos Cross with Stacy.

"Matt and I were talking yesterday as we headed to talk to Eddie. We discussed the possibility that the serious player might be Nikos Cross or at least someone who works for him."

Stacy's reaction was predictable, as she had gotten to know him during the case involving my ex-wife. "That motherfucker tried to kill you," she said to Matt. "He only got off because you couldn't remember who hit you and Cross blamed it on Georgi."

"See. We need to find a way to shake things up in order to get them to do something dumb. Any ideas."

There was just silence on the deck as we all thought about it.

Stacy was the first to speak. "Matt, you are an insurance investigator working on the fire at the Mockingbird. Anything you can think of about the fire that might point you toward Nikos Cross?"

Matt thought for a minute and offered, "I can't think about anything related to the fire but I have a friend who works for immigration and he might be able to give us some info on the human trafficking angle. This can't be the first time girls have been used by strip clubs then forced into porn and prostitution. I'll call him."

"Sounds good. Stacy could you check with OJ and see if he can share any information on strippers being arrested, who posts bail, who pays the legal fees and anything else we should be asking. We have tourists complaining at least once a month about the clubs overcharging for services *not* rendered."

"Got it," she agreed.

"I will check with the hospital to see if our John Doe is

awake and ready to talk after his close call with a sniper's bullet. I'm sure he knows more than he has said so far."

We agreed to meet for happy hour at the Mockingbird to check on progress and see how Abacus was doing.

~ ~ ~

My call to the hospital proved frustrating as the nurse covering the ER said Mr. Doe was having a CT scan to determine the extent of his injuries and no, his doctor reported he had not regained consciousness so I would not be able to talk to him.

I decided to walk Crutch down to the Southernmost Café for a Bloody Mary and to get the first exercise other than last night in a while. A swim out to the buoy and back would do me good assuming my leg would make it. After last night's calisthenics, I figured it would.

My phone rang and when I picked it up it was OJ.

"Finn, where are you?" he asked hurriedly.

"Headed for the beach for a swim and Bloody Mary, why?"

"Put it on hold and I'll pick you up at Duval and South in five minutes." And he hung up before I could get an answer.

As we walked back toward South Street from the beach, his car pulled up.

"Dude, what is this about?" I asked as he jumped out of his car.

"Finn, something has happened to Stacy," he said looking distressed.

"What?" I asked forcefully.

"We're not sure, but we think she's been taken."

Chapter Sixteen

"WHAT DO YOU mean taken? Taken where?"

"We're not sure Finn. We got a 911 from a tourist at Simonton by Ocean Wellness on Olivia who reported a girl being pulled into a van. Her bike was left behind on the street. We got there within four minutes but the van had already been abandoned about six blocks up Olivia near the cemetery. Stacy's purse was in the van but we don't know what vehicle was used after that."

"Are you sure it was her?" I asked as we took off.

"We checked the bike registration number from old records and it was her bike."

"So where to now?" I could barely get the question out as I was shaking so badly.

"We have set up a road block at Cow Key Channel Bridge and with luck we can catch them before they leave the island."

"Forget it. They would need to be idiots to leave that way. We need to cover the marinas and channels because they will leave by boat."

"Shit, you're probably right but there is no way we can stop every boat."

"They will use a powerboat. Fast, with long-range tanks and closed cabin, thirty five to forty feet long and ocean going. They will probably head toward Miami to get lost in all the Keys along the way. Also, check every private aircraft with a flight plan to leave in the next hour. They could try to fly her out as well."

"Finn," OJ asked with a low voice. "Who are *they*? Do you have any idea who we need to be looking for?"

"OJ, get this stuff organized first, then we can talk."

He got on the radio and began issuing orders based on my suggestions. He was mobilizing most of the cops on the island as well as Homeland Security and the Coast Guard.

In any kidnapping, the first few hours are the most critical in order to catch the kidnappers and bring the victim back safely and in one piece.

My phone rang and Stacy's number appeared. "Stacy?" I asked.

"No Meester Peelaar, you don't know me but I am a . . . ," he paused, "An acquaintance of your friend Stacy."

I didn't say a word but my stomach sank. He was clearly Czech or Bulgarian, perhaps Romanian.

In his heavy accent he said, "Meester Peelaar, your friend Stacy will be staying with us for a few days and she wishes me to tell you that you need not worry for her safety provided you follow my instructions."

"Listen asshole, if you touch a hair on her head, I'll hunt you down and cut your heart out with a spoon!" I could not believe I was channeling my inner Alan Rickman from Robin Hood-Prince of Thieves.

"Excuse me?" he asked.

"I will kill you if you touch her motherfucker."

"Whatever," he said, "Now *you* listen carefully."

"Fuck you!" I growled and hung up.

OJ was looking at me like I was nuts and I said to him, "Try to put a trace on the next call to come in on my phone and I stepped outside the car as the phone rang again.

"What?" I answered with a clearly short and pissed off tone.

In a calm voice, the same man said "Meester Peelaar, the next time you hang up on me I will leave an index finger from the beautiful Stacy's right hand in a small box addressed to you. Am . . . I . . . clear?"

I paused.

"Am . . . I . . . . Clear Meester Peelaar? You have lost several people you know in the last several days and you almost lost your life last night. Nice move with the dive tank and your friend, what's his name? Deevine? Appropriate I think," and then he paused for emphasis, "Am . . . I . . . clear?"

"Yes" I choked through gritted teeth.

"Good. Now you and Meester Deevine will spend the next few days working diligently on your bar with the silly name; the MockingBoar or the MockingButt." He chuckled.

"You will cease your inquiries into the activities involving Meester Hornet and any of his business interests. Am . . . I . . . clear?"

Fuck. Again with the repetition?

"Yes" I replied dutifully.

"Good. I will be in touch," and he hung up.

"Shit, we couldn't get a lock on the phone. Sorry Finn," said OJ.

This asshole had a flair for the melodramatic but I don't think he's bluffing. He never raised his voice and he knew about the events of the last several days including the explosion on the boat and our little diversion with the dive tank to rescue Eddie. He seems two steps ahead of us and then some.

I slumped back into OJ's car and called Matt who listened carefully as I walked him through my conversation with - I needed a good name for him - *Boris* worked. It helped me picture him as a cartoon character in his little black fedora, black suit and tiny mustache.

~ ~ ~

So now what, I thought. We're boxed in. He seems to know our every move and he's trying to keep us focused on the bar and away from Stinger. Why all the effort to protect semi legal strippers unless there was a bigger deal than even we suspected was going on?

In every case, you need to consider the four basic motives of any crime: Lust, Loathing, Lucre and Love. At this point, it seemed like this was about lust and lucre but it felt like we were missing something.

Again I was beginning to wonder if this might have been a simple case of drugs and sex that morphed into human trafficking and porn then into something more when Stacy unwittingly got me involved.

The only people I could think of who loathed me to this degree were already dead, with the exception of one.

Nikos Cross; the father of a dead son killed by me.

It appears that the human trafficking, prostitution, and pornography operations may be simply more threads in the web of Cross's criminal enterprise, in addition to drugs and money laundering. Now he may be the one holding the woman I love. *Wait. Did I just say the woman I love?*

I realized that Stacy had crept into my life gradually and unexpectedly and she had captured my wounded heart. Now she was in grave danger and I had no idea how to get her back. My moment of anxiety threatened to become a full-blown panic attack. I needed help but Matt was in the same box I was in, unable to act without harming Stacy.

I needed leverage then I needed to test the leash that Boris had put on us and locate Stacy. I turned to OJ.

"I need you to drive me to the Mockingbird then drop me off and drive away. I will go inside and call you."

"What are you thinking, Finn?" he asked.

"I have a couple of ideas but I am going to need you to appear uninvolved. Matt and I need to comply with the demands of the assholes holding Stacy or at least *appear to comply.* I'll call you in twenty minutes."

I stepped out of the car and turning back said, "Fuck you, asshole! Just keep your nose out of my life!" and slammed the door and marched into the Mockingbird. OJ sat in the car looking stunned then drove off.

Matt was just pulling up and he followed me through the door. We greeted Abacus who was surprised to see us both coming into the bar.

"To what do I owe the pleasure of your company?" he began, but he could tell right away that something was wrong. "What's up?"

I took a minute to explain what had happened and what I needed to do.

"I am going to work an angle I am still working out to see if I can shake this whole thing loose. We are going to need to work from here and we will need you to act as a go between."

"OK, what do you need?" was all he asked.

"We're going to need a job to do that will allow us to disappear for thirty minutes at a time but with a purpose and we are going to need a place to work in private," I began.

Abacus sat quietly for a minute, then said, "You can see in the corner we have those liquor shelves stacked up ready to install. As you know Finn, one of the reasons we rented this place was it is one of only two buildings in Key West with an underground cellar."

I knew that this building and the Rum Bar across the street were actual Speakeasy's during prohibition and liquor was stored in their basements. We're turning this basement into a storage cellar as it does keep things cool even in the heat of our summers.

"You can haul the shelves down to the basement then work on them for thirty minutes or so then come up and get the next set. The cellar is also very private."

"Great idea Abacus!" I said excitedly. "I'd like you to go through the motions of instructing us about moving things down stairs and about building the shelves. Then we can get started."

For the next five minutes, we stood dutifully in the

window of the restaurant and Abacus waved his arms then pointed to the basement. He took us down through the trap door behind the bar to the cellar.

Once we hauled the first set of shelves down the stairs, I walked Matt through my plan. He smiled.

I began by calling OJ to explain what I was going to need him to do. "OJ, sorry about the fuck you asshole bit." Before I could continue he simply said, "No worries. I missed it at first but I realized you just needed to put some obvious distance between us."

"Oh and fuck you too," he laughed.

With the pleasantries done and the bromance back on track, I said, "In the next twenty four hours, I am going to need you to be ready to put a trace on calls from a phone that is potentially connected to this crime. You will get an *anonymous tip* that a recent event is the beginning of a drug war between local drug gangs and you need a warrant."

He listened then asked, "What recent event?" He was sharp that way.

"One that may be occurring in the next few hours."

"Okaaay," he said slowly. I will go along with this idea for now but I will need details."

"All I can say is I want you to be able to trace a call between the two people I am trying to locate; one who is here in town and the other I suspect is holding Stacy hostage."

He agreed to get things in motion and to try to trace the call.

~ ~ ~

My last call was to an old buddy of mine who served with me in Iraq and was my partner in EOD. Sean (Boomer) Roberts was a fellow BUD/S dud meaning someone who did not complete BUD/S training (Basic Underwater Demolition/SEALS). In EOD, we all had handles like Boomer, Short Fuse or Shrapnel; mine had been Finn-alley.

All a bit gallows humor but in Spec Ops it was funny given the nature of the work.

Sean had classed up behind me and eventually followed the EOD route as well. During our first tour in Iraq together he was working on an IED that was blocking a convoy when we were ambushed by a bunch of Al-Qaeda assholes.

He was shot in the leg and bleeding badly but I was able to drag him into a ditch before the IED was lit off, probably by a garage door opener that at the time was one of the more popular remote triggering devices for setting them off. He always gave me credit for saving his life and the Navy saw fit to give me a Bronze Star for what was in my view just me dragging him, as we scrambled for cover.

Personally I think every Navy SEAL deserves a medal for just doing what they do. Mine was just self-preservation using a friend for cover.

Sean always said if I ever needed help to call him and I couldn't think of a time when I needed help more.

"Hey Boomer, it's Finn-alley."

"Well, I'll be damned. How you been bro?"

"Honestly man, I would love to catch up but I am in a spot and could use a favor."

"Anything man, what do you need?" he offered freely.

"Well it will involve the use of your old skills dude. I need to create some havoc."

"As long as I don't have to kill anybody, I am your man," he chuckled. "You know my motto dude; *Cry havoc and let slip the dogs of war.*"

Boomer and I use to trade quotes from Shakespeare in our down time in the sandbox. It's funny how it comes back so quickly.

I laughed and offered back, "*and I assume the port of Mars; and at my heels, leash'd in like hounds, should famine, sword and fire crouch for employment.*"

"You always did have a thing for Henry V," he chucked

then got serious. "What do you need?" and I explained what I wanted.

"While you talked, I have been online checking flights and I can be there in eight hours. That work for you?"

"Perfect" I said. "I'll get what you'll need and have it ready for you."

"Don't bother, you have enough to worry about. I have everything I need and can check it with no problem."

"Thanks so much Boomer" I said gratefully.

"No man, thank *you* for the chance to return the favor I owe you. You know this one I think," then quoted from the St. Crispin Day speech, "*We few, we happy few, we band of brothers; For he today that sheds his blood with me shall be my brother.*" And he hung up before we got all blubbery.

BUD/S even for those of us who did not make it through, was a trial by fire and many of us will be brothers for life.

With Boomer on the way and Matt and I stuck for the moment, I had two more calls to make.

Chapter Seventeen

"LOWER KEYS MEDICAL, Rosa speaking. How can I help you?"

My lucky day. "Hi Rosa, it's Finn Pilar calling. How are you?"

"Hey Finn. I'm good, how about you? You finish your rehab yet?"

No, not that kind of rehab. It's a small town and Rosa and I were in physical therapy together after I was shot in the shoulder. Who knew that finding a square grouper on the beach would result in such an injury?

"Yes, thanks for asking. I got a clean bill of health a month ago. My shoulder is still a bit stiff but usually only if it's going to rain. And you?"

"Going well. I feel like the Bionic Woman but it's all good.

"Rosa, it's great to catch up. Can you please transfer me up to the ER? I want to check on a patient who came in last night."

"Sure, Finn here you go."

"ER." answered a curt and harried voice.

"You have a John Doe that came in last night with a possible concussion. Can you tell me if he is conscious yet and talking?"

She paused and I could hear papers shuffling. "John Doe? No he is still unconscious and he has a serious concussion so we are keeping him sedated. Who is this?" she asked.

"My name is Finn Pilar and I brought him in last night. Thanks for the update," and I hung up.

I walked back up to the window in the bar and picked

up another box of shelving to take down to the basement.

Matt and I ate lunch at La Te Da across the street from the Mockingbird as our kitchen was not quite ready.

In the military, we were taught to seize the initiative but until Boomer got into town, we could take little action. I had no idea how Boris was tracking us and I didn't want to do anything that might put Stacy at risk until I was in a position to put pressure on Cross. The waiting is the hardest part.

After returning to the Mockingbird, my phone rang.

"Meester Pilar, I hope you enjoyed your lunch at La Te Da," he oozed with venom.

Son of a bitch. This asshole has us covered tighter than a gnat's ass. How is he doing it? Nothing was obvious.

"Look asshole, I told you I would follow along but if you as much as touch a hair on her head, I will hunt you down and I will kill you," I retorted.

"Really Meester Peelaar? There is no need for so much, how you Americans say, *drama*. We are both professionals and this is just business. I simply want you to know that if you deviate from the agreed program, then your friend will be returned to you in pieces."

"Am . . I . . . Clear?"

"Yes, you are clear," I responded but he had hung up. Asshole.

Matt and I continued our routine. About every half hour we would take another set of shelves down to the basement then talk about our next steps.

The hours went by like Chinese water torture, a drip at a time.

Just before six o'clock p.m., Boomer called. "Hey Finn-Alley, I'm leaving the airport and I have a reservation at the Westin like you suggested. I should be there in about fifteen minutes."

We discussed the final details. We would wait until dark

to swing into action.

I called OJ and gave him the number that I wanted him to trace beginning at eight-thirty that night.

"Whose number is it?" he asked.

"Are you sure you want to know?" I replied.

"Well I have the warrant for the number but it would help to have a name in case they have more than one number."

I thought about this and said, "Nikos Cross."

"Oh shit Finn. You are kidding right? This guy is untouchable."

"I told you that you might not want to know."

"Finn, my ass is now on the line."

"OJ, believe me after tonight, you'll be a hero. Just remember, you got a tip about a possible feud between rival drug gangs from an anonymous source so you put the tap on. If what I think is true you will be a star."

OJ continued to grumble about his career, his future children and how he would make a living if he lost his job or worse, went to jail.

"Dude, man up. You never planned on having kids and you're not even married. I got to go. Just start to monitor the number at eight p.m." I hung up.

Matt and I decided we would head over to Martin's with Abacus for a cocktail and dinner. Martin's is my go to spot for happy hour but dinner is also spectacular. We were too late for the happy hour deals but we had an hour to kill so food seemed in order.

With Stacy being held hostage and the first phase of my plan about to kick off, food became simply fuel. I had the grouper and a glass of Rombauer but left both half eaten. Actually I did finish the wine as it was too good to go to waste.

At exactly eight p.m. I got a text from Sean. A simple '?' to which I replied 'Y'.

As we headed back to the Mockingbird I stopped and picked up a cigar at the shop next to Denny's. We walked slowly toward the bar as I fired up a Robusto.

We could hear the explosion faintly in the distance and some people on the street looked to the sky thinking it might be an approaching storm. I knew what it was, and it was not what they were thinking.

We got back to the Mockingbird and waited.

After fifteen minutes, my phone rang.

"Meester Peelaar, I would like you to hear the results of your little, shall I say, feeble attempt at gaining leverage."

The scream I heard next was like nothing I had ever experienced.

Chapter Eighteen

I HAD HEARD MEN WOUNDED in combat scream, and while chilling it is expected.

But when someone you love is being violated, it hits you in a place you cannot describe. Your skin feel like it's on fire and your heart seems to stop beating.

"WHAT THE FUCK ARE YOU TALKING ABOUT?" I screamed. "STOP!"

"Meester Peelaar, any other attempt to get in the way of our operation will result in her death in a very unpleasant fashion. You will be getting a package in the mail shortly. Am . . . I . . . clear?" he snarled.

"If you've hurt her, I *will* kill you. Am . . . I . . . clear asshole?" and I hung up first so I could feel a semblance of control.

I took a couple of deep breaths and tried to calm the adrenaline pumping through my system. *Have I just cost Stacy her life?*

I jumped when my phone rang again. It was OJ.

"What the fuck did you do Finn?" he shouted.

I took another deep breath. "OJ, what are you talking about? I am sitting in the Mockingbird with a cigar after a meal at Martin's with Matt and Abacus."

"You know exactly what I am talking about. A go fast boat docked at Cross's house on Sunset Key blew up tonight taking most of the dock with it, the windows of his house and the ones closest to it."

I guess Sean must have used a little too much C4.

"I did warn you that a feud between drug dealers might get out of hand."

"Finn, if I ever find out you had a hand in this, I will

159

string you up by your thumbs and cut your nuts off with a fork."

"Dude, where did that one come from? I mean a *fork*? What happened with the trace?"

He paused and seemed to collect himself, "Yeah, the trace. That was weird. Right after the explosion, a call on the line went out to a cell phone located in the Bahamas, some small island in the middle of nowhere. I'm amazed they even have cell service"

"Where OJ, where?" I asked breathlessly.

"It's some place called Lee Stocking Island. It was such an odd name, I googled it. There is an abandoned NOAA base there with a thousand meter long airstrip."

I hung up and called Boomer while Matt went online and got the coordinates of the island and took a couple of screen shots on Google Earth so we could get the lay of the land. It was not the level of detail we used to get before an operation in the teams, but it would have to do.

"Nice job Boomer, maybe a bit over the top with the C4 but nice work."

"You said create *havoc* man," he chuckled, "So I thought a little more is better."

I could feel his big crooked smile coming through the phone. I had briefed Boomer on the go fast boat that Cross kept at his dock at Sunset Key, the small luxury residential island about five hundred yards off the coast of Key West. The Cross compound sat on the shore facing the Westin hotel near the navy pier.

Boomer as a former EOD diver had no problem navigating the currents in the Key West channel during slack tide and I had warned him about potential boat security measures I had discovered on a previous dive. I asked him to make sure no one was near the boat, then attach a block of C4 explosive to the hull and blow it at eight thirty.

My objective was to force Cross to call his guy who I assumed was the guy I called *Boris,* to find out what the hell was going on. By having OJ trace the call I hoped to locate Stacy. Matt and I stayed visible at the Mockingbird so we would have plausible deniability and hopefully minimize any risk to her. *As it turned out, hope is not a strategy.*

My plan worked for the most part but like any plan, there can be unintended consequences; namely Stacy may have been hurt. I hated to think about it but I could see no other way to find out where she was being held.

"Ok Boomer time for Phase Two," I told him and hung up.

Matt and I left the window of the Mockingbird and went down to the cellar carrying the last of the shelving. Having established that pattern all day, I figured it would buy us between thirty to forty minutes before he became suspicious. If he tried to call me, he would not get an answer.

What Boris was unlikely to know, is as a former prohibition speakeasy, the cellar had to be prepared for a raid at any time. The patrons needed a way to escape during a raid and so the owners had built a passage out of the cellar and into the hotel next door. Boarded up when we took it over, we thought it would be a unique feature for folks staying at the hotel to be able to come underground into the Mockingbird for a drink. We scurried through the passage and into the hotel next door.

I had arranged for a cab to meet us at the hotel and we walked out holding hands and pretending to be a gay couple all kissy face as we got into the cab.

Matt said, "Come on dude, we agreed no tongues." I laughed to ease the tension I felt as we tried to slip the surveillance Boris clearly had on us.

"Let's hope Boris is homophobic and doesn't want to watch a gay couple making out and getting into a cab."

Tequila Mockingbird

"I get that," Matt said, "but you seemed to enjoy it."

"Any port in a storm man." I tried to keep our spirits up. We headed to the airport where we were meeting Boomer.

Boomer was there waiting for us as we pulled into the private terminal. When he came into town, he had arranged to charter a Cessna 208A Caravan from the Banzai Jump School Key West. The Caravan has a range of about nine hundred miles and a speed of about three hundred and fifty miles as hour. We figured that would be enough for almost anywhere we needed to go.

~ ~ ~

Banzai is owned by a former SEAL operator and teammate of Matt's, Will Morimoto, who was a member of the Navy SEAL Leap Frogs program in the late 90's. He retired to the Keys and had his school on Sugarloaf around mile marker twenty. Matt arranged for Will to come down to meet us, then fly us wherever we needed to go.

We piled into the Caravan and began checking the gear as Will got clearance and we took off. He brought three Ram Air Canopy chutes, an M91A2 Sniper rifle and two Sig Sauer P226s from his personal collection. I had my own USP .40.

Will also handed us each a combat radio with throat mics and Recon-1 tactical knife. I gave him the coordinates of the island and figured it would take us about an hour to cover the three hundred miles.

Our published flight plan was to George Town, in the Exumas at an altitude of twenty thousand feet. We would drop down to fifteen thousand as we approached Lee Stocking and do a HA/HO jump about a mile from the island. HA/HO jumps are High Altitude/High Opening jumps designed to allow troops to jump then basically travel for a distance of up to thirty miles across the ground to a drop zone.

We were only jumping from fifteen thousand feet so a couple of miles was about our range. We would glide onto the abandoned airfield we could see on the Google Earth screen shots Matt took. It appeared to be out of sight of the compound on the water near the old NOAA base.

As we took off, my phone rang and it was Stacy's number. I ignored it but knew it would be Boris and the clock had started ticking.

Will took off and we began climbing to our twenty thousand foot altitude heading almost due east to George Town. I figured we were an hour and half out from our drop at the airstrip and two hours from reaching Stacy. My old instincts and adrenaline began to kick in.

I knew that Boris would keep trying to reach me and at some point would figure that we were up to something and might move Stacy. We needed to move fast.

Will went full throttle to get us there and fifty-five minutes after we took off we were in range of the island. Air traffic control (ATC) was beginning to ask why we were off course and Will then reported a problem with his GPS. Given the problems with drug smuggling in the past, ATC is very sensitive to an aircraft off course. Will then reported engine trouble and requested a lower altitude to look for a place to land.

He had timed it perfectly to get us down to fifteen thousand feet right were we wanted to drop. We were suited up and able to exit the Caravan quickly through the large door. We dropped as a group and waited a few seconds before pulling our chutes then began floating toward the abandoned airstrip. From about five thousand feet we could see light coming from of one of the houses in the old NOAA Research Station that presumably had been abandoned after the crash of 2007. I was betting that Stacy was being held there.

Will would continue to fly in wide circles about a mile off the shore of the island claiming to be looking for a place to safely set down while we went after Stacy.

As we continued to spiral down getting closer to the ground we looked for signs of any additional hostiles. The usual giveaways are careless smokers who light up revealing their position or the flashlight to search an abandoned building. Fortunately the moon was low on the horizon and at its lowest point in the waning cycle so was only a sliver on the horizon. Either Boris ran a very tight crew or he was alone.

After landing on the runway, we gathered our chutes and put them in a dilapidated Quonset hut that seemed to have been used to store old supplies. We then followed a dirt road and climbed up a small hill to survey the NOAA site below.

In low voices, we discussed our plan.

"Matt, if you look at this site, it is going to be tough to get to it from here. The road goes over a small bridge that is a natural choke point that Boris is sure to be covering. He may have night vision goggles and we are literally operating in the dark except for the scope on the M91."

"That about sums it up Finn," Matt replied. "Just the way I like it."

"Boomer, we need to have you on overwatch. You take the M91 and head over to the trees on this side of the bridge where you can get a clear shot at the house with the lights on."

"I will click twice on the radio after we have reached the compound and can be sure Boris is not lined up to shoot anyone crossing the bridge."

"Roger that," he replied. Old habits die hard as we once more were executing a mission together.

"Matt, you take the salt pond on the right and use the concrete pens for cover to cross to the first building on the right. I will go around the pond on the left bank and work my way to the other side of the building with the lights."

"Got it," he said.

"Once we get to the compound, Boomer you cross the bridge and join Matt by the first building but watch for mines on the bridge. This guy has a history of using explosives."

"You're a bundle of laughs, Finn," said Boomer. "Bombs, it had to be bombs. You know I hate bombs. Why do I always get the bombs?" Given his work in EOD we all chuckled, then headed out.

I stayed close to the shore of the salt pond wading through muck and mangrove roots which made for slow going. Once Matt dropped into the ditch beside the road then into the concrete pens that used to hold fish when the place was an operational research center, he disappeared.

I continued to slog around the pond but after about fifteen minutes I heard Matt click once on the radio to let us know he was in position by the first building. It took me another five minutes to reach a small hill overlooking the house with the lights. I clicked twice to let Boomer know we were in position. I could see no movement but I could see a big go fast boat with three outboard engines floating at the dock.

I waited as Boomer crossed the bridge uneventfully and paired up with Matt. I knew they were moving into position to cover two sides of the house.

Suddenly with a flash of light the house exploded and I was sent flying back about thirty feet. *This guy really likes bombs* I thought as I was in the air. I knew Matt and Boomer were also probably in the air but where the hell were Boris and Stacy?

The explosion had caused me to lose my hearing at least momentarily, as I am sure it did the others. I quickly looked around to see if I could see Boris.

Out of the corner of my eye I caught a glimpse of someone running toward the go fast boat about thirty yards away. I raised my gun, and fired. The runner stumbled, continue on a step or two then fell. I looked at my gun as if to say, *damn, I was never that good a shot.*

I looked around and saw Boomer with the rifle pointed at the guy I believed to be Boris. I waved. Now where had the guy come from? I looked around again and could just make out a small building like a tool shed past a small rocky outcrop. Could Stacy be in there?

I began to go over to check when another explosion and shock wave knocked me down. Pieces of the guy on the ground who Boomer had shot came raining down and as I turned looking for Boomer I saw him on the ground not moving. *Fuck.*

Boomer appeared to have been going over to check on the guy on the ground when the guy exploded. I ran over to Boomer to check for a pulse and it was there, faint, but there. He was bleeding from his shoulder and his forehead. I stuck a tampon in the shoulder wound as Matt came up beside me. So why do I carry ultra-absorbency tampons? They can absorb up to eighteen grams of blood, fit great in a wound and easy to apply pressure. *It's amazing what you learn on the battlefield.*

A quick check by Matt and he mouthed the word, "Fine," and pointed toward the shed.

So far we had been hit with two bombs and still no sign of Stacy. It was time to hit the shed. We each moved left to be behind the rock outcrop as we approached the doorway.

Matt took one side of the door and I took the other. He turned the knob and then I pushed the door open with the barrel of my gun.

Sitting taped on an upright wooden chair with her back to us was Stacy. She had a note taped to her back that mockingly said, "Bomb. Am ... I ... Clear?"

Chapter Nineteen

AS MATT AND I CIRCLED the chair from each side, Stacy's face came into view. Even with her mouth taped shut, you could tell she was terrified. The whites of her eyes were showing fully as she screamed silently at me. A quick check of her hands showed that Boris had not cut off her finger as promised.

Slowly I reached up and put my finger to my lips in the universal sign of *be quiet*. She paused and seemed to get control. Slowly I pulled the duct tape from her mouth using the same finger, trying to minimize the pain. "Thank God you found me," she cried. "Now cut me the fuck loose. I want to kill that asshole if you haven't already!"

I took my time to reply. "Stacy, there is a note on your back that says *Bomb*. I want to check it first before I let you move." Her face froze.

I lowered myself onto the floor to look under the chair and saw something that turned my stomach. Stacy was sitting on a bomb made with C4 and it had a pressure plate trigger, a timer and a cell phone trigger.

Sure make it simple. I had three chances of getting it wrong.

In the distance I heard an engine fire up and rev to maximum power. Matt rushed out of the room and I could hear gunshots in rapid succession until I imagine the clip was empty, then a second or two later another clip being emptied, one round after the other.

I stayed with Stacy but I knew our time was limited. If the cell phone was used to trigger the bomb, we were all dead in a matter of seconds.

I pulled out my Leatherman that every EOD tech carries

167

as a matter of course. The basics of defusing a bomb, is never do what I was about to do. The movies usually get it wrong but most of the time we use a device called a PAN disruptor. It is a device very much like a shotgun in that it fires a projectile that remotely detonates the bomb.

For obvious reasons that is not an option in this case so I will be forced to fall back on the movie solution of locating and cutting the wires connecting the trigger to the blasting cap embedded in the C4.

The trigger in each case is a device that sends a charge to the blasting cap causing it to explode and then detonate the larger charge of C4. It is sort of like putting your tongue on both terminals of a 9-volt battery and you get a shock from the current if the battery is good.

Each of the triggers on this bomb could be used to close the circuit and detonate it. I had no idea which one to start with first. There was no convenient countdown clock on the timer but I knew as long as Stacy didn't stand up, the pressure plate was safe. Having said that, getting her out was my priority so I started there.

"Stacy, I am going to cut the duct tape holding you to the chair but please don't get up until I tell you to or we may both be meeting again in some other world. I will then cut the trigger wire to the pressure plate that you are sitting on. I will then tell you to get up and slowly walk out of the building. Understood?"

In a surprisingly calm voice she said, "Get me the fuck off this thing!" OK, maybe not so calm but under the circumstances, icy.

"It's going to be fine. Remember I did this for a living."

"You're more nuts that I thought, but get on with it. I need to pee," she chuckled.

I looked down at my hands to see them shaking and I knew there was a reason I got out of this line of work.

After cutting the tape from Stacy's arms and legs I lay

back down on my side to look up under the chair and begin tracing the wires. I realized on closer inspection that the trigger wires were twisted around each other so it was impossible to tell which wire was connected to which trigger. *Thanks asshole for making this so simple.*

After about two minutes looking for any hidden circuits or additional triggers, I decided I had no choice but to cut them all at once. Using the wire cutters on the Leatherman I reached up and placed them on the twist of wire. I counted to three, held my breath and cut.

The explosion that followed was only in my head as I flashed to a time I lost a fellow EOD tech in Afghanistan. He was doing a similar job trying to defuse a bomb on a local Afghan tribesman who had C4 strapped to his neck. When the tech cut the wire to the countdown clock on the guy's chest, it sent a signal to a cell phone that was then used to detonate the bomb remotely.

Once my heart restarted in my chest, I collectedly told Stacy to calmly walk out of the shed door then run as fast as she could toward the other side of the compound. Then she could pee.

"Stacy, stand up very slowly, walk to the door, then run like hell."

"What about you?" she asked.

"I'll race you to the bridge," I replied with a smile.

As I stood up to leave, I heard the cell phone ring under the chair. I paused, then reached down and answered it. "Fuck you asshole," I began.

After a second he replied, "Congratulations Meester Peelaar. I hope to see you and Miss. Barnett again very soon. Am . . . I . . . Clear?" and he hung up. I had heard the sound of outboards in the background and he was full throttle heading somewhere.

"This guy Boris is getting on my nerves," I muttered to myself as I walked out the door and looked across the compound to see Stacy and Matt working on Boomer. He was sitting up and swearing like a sailor as he looked at the M91 that had been damaged by a piece of shrapnel from the bomb that must have been strapped to the guy who ran out of the shed.

"You're supposed to *defuse* the bombs Boomer. Blocking the shrapnel after the fact isn't part of the training is it?"

"It's part of the advanced course, Finn-alley. You flunked that part remember?"

Clearly he was feeling better and only a little damaged. At this point my cell rang again and Will came on.

"You never write. You never call. Are you kids finished playing and ready to go home?" he asked.

Shit I had forgotten he was flying around pretending to be on the verge of crashing as far as ATC was concerned.

"Yeah, we have one cowboy a little worse for wear and the Indians got away but we saved the rancher's daughter so I'd say we're done here," I replied.

"Ok, the cavalry is on the way. Can you light a small fire at each end of the runway and make sure nothing's growing in the middle of it to get in my way. I'll do another circuit and be there in ten minutes."

"Got it," I replied

Matt took off to light the fires and check the runway while Stacy and I helped Boomer up and supported him as the three of us walked slowly back to the airstrip.

By the time we got across the bridge and started up the hill, we could see Will on final approach then circle around and headed back toward us as we reached the edge of the airstrip.

We had ditched the M91 and the three pistols in the salt pond as we crossed the bridge knowing we would be inspected when we landed. We piled into the Caravan while Will radioed that he had landed safely on some island with an abandoned airstrip to affect repairs. We waited about twenty minutes bringing him up to speed on the night's events then we requested permission to resume our flight plan to George Town. We were instructed to report directly to Customs and Immigration for inspection upon arrival.

We arrived at the George Town Airport and were greeted by the entire six man police force with their drug sniffing dog who proceeded to tear apart the aircraft. By the time they finished, the sun was coming up over the horizon.

We did not have time to spend on the island even for breakfast. One of my favorite restaurants in the Exumas is *Catch a Fire Sunset Bar and Grill* that has not only great food, music and drinks, but one of the best sunset views you will ever see.

I needed to remember to take Stacy there once this whole kidnapped, held hostage, and almost blown up by a bomb experience was less fresh in her mind.

We finally cleared Bahamas Customs and Immigration and our flight back to Key West proved uneventful.

While Boomer rested in the back of the plane I had a chance to reflect on our little sojourn to Lee Stocking Island.

"Stacy, one question," I began. "Who was the guy who came running out of the tool shed and then got blown up?"

"You know that is a good question. I never saw him but I heard voices in a foreign language. The guy you called Boris introduced himself to me as Vladimir. The other one never gave a name nor did he seem to speak English."

"Well given that Vladimir strapped a bomb to him and then blew it up, it seems he was not too important a player in this mess."

"Did you get any idea who might be behind any of this while Vlad held you hostage?" I asked.

"No, the only thing I can tell you is that when a call came in earlier this evening, he first spoke English on the phone and he was really pissed. After he hung up, he ranted and raved in Russian.

He went out for about an hour and came back with the bomb for my chair." After thinking for a minute, she then added, "The only other thing I saw was a bank of computer monitors in the house that got blown up. When he first took me there, he told me that I should not expect a rescue as he was monitoring you and Matt using the web cams all over the city."

"Well that explained how he could tell what we were doing. So how did he get you to scream?" I asked.

"I am not proud of it," she replied lowering her voice slightly. "He took a nail file and stuck it under my thumb nail. You have no idea how much that hurts."

I did, but I wasn't going to get into it with her.

"Babe, I am so sorry you got caught up in this mess. I truly am."

"Finn, it's not your fault," she said. "I was the one that got you into it to begin with because of Trixie," and she started to cry. It was the first visible sign of the stress she had been under. I put my arm around her and she continued to silently weep, her shoulders shuddering and tears flowing.

After a few minutes I said, "You know Stacy, I'm not sure. It may have started with Trixie but I've had a feeling for a while that there's more to this situation than meets the eye."

"What are you th . . th . . . thinking?" she sniffed.

"Well, you may not like this but in order to find you, I needed to take some risks. You know I had a hunch that Nikos Cross was involved somehow. I decided to stir the pot and had Boomer create a little chaos."

"What kind of chaos?" she asked.

"Not important," I said. "I had OJ monitor Cross's cell phone and when he called Vlad, we were able to pinpoint your location. Unfortunately it also triggered Vlad to make you scream to get me under control. In the end my plan worked but it did put you at risk."

"So what, you're saying is that Cross is behind this whole thing and it's about you killing his son?" she inquired.

"Well I don't know and can't prove anything, but he clearly seems to be involved. He placed a call to Vlad after we blew up his boat. He hired Vlad probably from the same place as his last bodyguard Georgi and he does have a motive; I killed his son."

"Wait," she replied curtly. You blew up his boat?"

"Well *I* didn't personally do it, but let's just say I spit balled the idea with someone who took it upon themselves to do it."

Stacy frowned then shook her head. She turned toward me and kissed me. "Thank you," she said sweetly and smiled.

We landed at Key West and after a cursory inspection, caught a cab back to Catherine Street. I called Abacus and invited him to join us at La Petite Paris for breakfast. After an order of their incredible Lobster Benedict with extra Hollandaise for everyone, we shared the update with Abacus and crammed some calories.

Satiated after a long night, we headed home. After taking a look at Boomer's shoulder, cleaning it up and applying a fresh dressing he crashed on the couch after downing a couple of Advils. Matt climbed to the loft and Stacy and I retired to the bedroom. *Ownership has its privileges.*

~ ~ ~

It seemed that life quieted down after our return from the Bahamas. Abacus and Rico made great progress over the next week toward cleaning up and repairing the Mockingbird and a call to Bobby let me know we had fifteen entrants for our *Key West Porn Idol* competition. The grand opening of the Mockingbird was set for the week of Fantasy

Fest now just three days away.

Boomer stayed with us for the week and we spent most evenings swapping tales of our friends no longer with us. We sampled food and drink at the best restaurants in town in preparation for designing the menu for the Mockingbird. We were working on a theme of Mexican and Southern like Southern Fried Burritos, Enchiladas with Collard Greens and Pecan Pie with a Reposado Tequila sauce.

Stacy stayed for a few days but needed to get back to work in Tampa. She promised to return for *Key West Porn Idol* and be a judge. Boomer headed back to Virginia Beach where he had settled after leaving the Navy and Matt returned to Miami.

Life seemed to be settling down but something just didn't feel right. I had a feeling this was the calm before the storm.

Crutch and I felt like the only ones not voted off the island. We restarted our morning routine with a ride around the island, a Bloody at Southernmost and a swim to the buoy and back. We had finally gotten the insurance money for the fire and were able to replace the furniture and restock the bar.

I stayed in touch with OJ but there was no fresh news on the bombings of the strip club nor the trailer. I also discovered that Eddie had been released in the afternoon before we flew to Lee Stocking Island and had not been seen since.

Chapter Twenty

I REALLY WANTED to get something special for the opening of the Mockingbird to attract crowds and make a name for ourselves as *the* place to go for Tequila.

I decided it was time to call my good friend Ricardo Ramos whose family had been in the Tequila business for seven generations. The family owned a three thousand acre plantation growing Blue Agave, the primary ingredient in high quality tequila. They also had a manufacturing operation to render agave, crush it, ferment the juice, distill it and bottle it. I had gotten to know Ricardo during the drug wars in Mexico when he invited a team of SEAL contractors to come down to his ranch to help train his security personnel. I was invited to work on bomb detection and disposal in the event of car bombs etc.

He and I hit it off when I found a bomb under his car that his team had missed while we were on a practice mission into the city. It wasn't a real bomb but his team missed it, so as far as he was concerned I had saved his life.

When we were leaving after a week, he took me aside and handed me a plain bottle with no label. It was the family's private stock of one hundred year old Tequila. Aged in the last Mexican white oak barrel still in use, it had been walled up during the repression of Christians in the early twentieth century and only rediscovered in the early 1980's. Each year the family draws five percent from the twenty-five hundred liter barrel for personal use and replenishes it with tequila made from the original recipe.

"Hola mi amigo. It's Finn Pilar."

"Eh Finn, como estas mi amigo. Que pasa?"

"It's a long story my friend. I won't bore you with the

details. How are you and Margarita?"

"We are muy bien mi amigo, even mi padre is doing great."

"I am delighted to hear it, and your team is obviously keeping you safe?" I joked.

"Si, they are," he replied. "So what's with you?"

I proceeded to give him the Reader's Digest version of events.

"Are you finally ready to accept my investment in the bar?" he inquired. "I never offer unless I am serious."

"Well I am, sort of . . . " I replied.

"What is this *sort of*?" he asked.

"Abacus and I have discussed this and we would like to invite you to become a partner in the bar with a ten percent share. In return, and I know this is a big ask, but we don't want your money."

"I am sorry my friend but I don't understand."

"We want your tequila."

"But Finn, you already can have my tequila through my U.S. distributor and I can arrange a friends and family discount for you. You don't need to give me a share for that," he replied.

"No, my friend, we want your family tequila; your private stock."

There was silence on the phone.

"We will give you ten percent of the bar for a quarter cask of the private stock each year and the exclusive rights in the U.S." The silence was deafening. "Ricardo, are you still there?" I asked.

"Yes, my friend, I am thinking."

I waited patiently and quietly - not my best virtues.

"Finn, but for you I would not be here today to have this discussion." He paused.

I waited. Good thing I was already on island time.

"I ask two things from you: the first that I can attend

the tapping of the cask each year; and that you and I will sip the first glass over a fine Cuban cigar. Oh and one more thing. Fifteen percent. Is it a deal?"

I laughed. "It is a deal my friend and thank you from the bottom of my heart. Oh and one more thing. Can you be here in three days with the cask?"

He laughed. "I will get them to warm up the Lear, pull the cask from the warehouse and see you tomorrow. Hasta luego mi amigo."

I did the math in my head. A quarter cask has eighty liters. Each liter is about twenty generous shots. At two hundred dollars a shot for the rarest tequila in the world sold under our Mockingbird brand, a bottle would retail at four thousand dollars so the quarter cask is worth over three hundred thousand. *Now that is a good day's work.*

~ ~ ~

It was a busy time for Abacus as I had given him all the last minute details launching the bar during Fantasy Fest. But I really missed Stacy and looked forward to her return for opening night along with Matt and Boomer.

I was so busy I almost forgot that Boris or Vlad - as I now properly called him - was still out there and I suspected Nikos Cross was plotting with him.

The day of the opening was a mad scramble to prepare. Ricardo had flown in the day before with the cask of liquid gold and the newspaper ads and flyers were all over town. It would be hard to be one of the fifty thousand visitors to Key West and not know about our event, the first annual *Key West Porn Idol* contest with the doors opening at five p.m. The ads boasted a free Tequila Fireball and the chance to vote for your favorite video along with the judges, J-Lo Nolower, Steven Tieher, and Semen Cowlick.

The line started to form about four p.m. and by five, it was a block long. The bar was full to overflowing and we had set up TV screens on the street for the competition and the crowd was getting rowdier by the minute.

J-Lo Nolower was played by a local transvestite named Q-Mitch for Queen Mitch who usually called bingo Sunday afternoons at the 801 Cabaret on Duval. When not calling bingo he worked at the ticket counter at the Key West Airport.

Steven Tieher was my favorite local eccentric who usually wears a tutu with matching fishnet stockings and a tiara.

To round out the team, Bobby from Bobby's Bodacious Booty Boutique insisted on playing Semen Cowlick. I of course, was Ryan See-crust, the host of the show.

"Ladies and gentleman," I began after introducing each of the judges to gales of laughter and applause from the assembled crowd. "Tonight we welcome you to the first annual *Key West Porn Idol* competition. We have scoured the four corners of the known ...*island* to select a group of ten finalists for our competition. After reviewing the twelve submissions, our judges selected these ten finalists. Two were really bad, so we eliminated them." Boos emanated from the audience.

"No I mean . . . really bad." Cheers erupted from the audience.

"The rules for tonight are as follows: we are handing out a scorecard with the titles of each of the ten films and a rating chart from one to five; we will play each of the three-minute films and you must rate each of them, one being Limp to five being Stiff. Each completed card will entitle you to a free Tequila Fireball. Are you ready?"

The crowd cheered.

"Our first film tonight is, "Debbie does Stock Island.""

The crowd roared as the screens inside and outside the bar lit up. Emerging from a local fish market, one of our local strippers slowly begins removing her clothes. The camera drew back for a wider shot to reveal a line of local fisherman. She then beckoned the first in line to join her in a corner of the parking lot as she knelt before him slowly unbuttoning his bib overalls. The camera then rises to his face as he grows more and more excited eventually making a clearly realistic O-face.

The crowd cheered, whistled or groaned as each of the next eight films were played.

Finally, I introduced the last film of the night, "Our final entry tonight is *Trailer Park Roulette*. The screens again light up.

This submission is clearly the one shot with Trixie with some heavy editing. It begins with Trixie and Rocco doing tequila shooters as she removes her clothes seductively in front of a clearly excited Rocco. Finally naked, they both lean over a table and appear to snort a white powder. She then lies across the table and Rocco approaches her doggy style and pulls out a gun from a drawer in the table.

The crowd who had been cheering unabashedly, collectively gasped and went silent.

Rocco does another shot of tequila, spins the chamber, points the gun at the back of her head and pulls the trigger. They both laugh then move to the bed and change positions so she is on top of him. He spins the chamber again and hands her the gun. He sprinkles more powder on her naked breasts, snorts it and does a third tequila shot. She begins to ride him as he bucks and squirms under her, yelling, now bitch, now! She points the gun and the screen goes dark.

The audience is deathly silent then erupts in cheers and total mayhem. OJ and I had no idea how this final film would be received but we were hoping it would allow us to declare it the winner and award it the ten thousand dollar prize in hopes of catching the killer.

Hard to do, but we both underestimated the audience during Fantasy Fest. Few if any, had any idea that it actually showed the lead up to a murder. Most were simply acknowledging the films suspense but it was a sick testament to the moral state of our world that it would be cheered.

Trying to maintain my enthusiasm in light of this insight, I called out, "Ladies and gentlemen, get your scorecards handed in and collect your free Tequila Fireball. Our judges will tabulate the results in the presence of our accounting firm Dewey, Take'm and How, then we will announce the winner at eight thirty. The winning filmmaker must be present this evening to collect the prize. In the meantime, drink up and enjoy your evening.

Our judges were in on the sting and after an hour of *tabulating* the results, they returned with a winner.

"Ladies and gentleman, we have a winner," I announced to cheers and hoots from the crowd.

"The winner of the first annual *Key West Porn Idol* is the film *Trailer Park Roulette*. Would the film-maker who produced this film, please come up and collect your ten thousand dollar check and our heartfelt congratulations."

The audience began searching around to see who would come forward but no one appeared.

"Again, would the producer of the film *Trailer Park Roulette* please come forward to collect your prize?" Still nothing.

I took a minute to confer with the judges then said, "The judges have agreed that we'll wait twenty four hours then if the prize is not claimed, we'll award it to the second place finisher.

To groans and hisses, we wrapped up the show and with Abacus working the bar, Stacy and I went back to the house to consider next steps. Matt and Ricardo decided to take in the sights of Fantasy Fest and headed to Mallory Square. Boomer still recovering from his injuries found a comfortable corner of the bar, ordered his favorite

Herradura Reposado and watched a particularly attractive brunette getting hit on at the bar. I had a feeling he might be going to her rescue at any moment.

~ ~ ~

We had not been able to break open the murder of Rocco with our Porn Idol contest and while we suspected it was Vlad, we still had no proof he killed Trixie, Squeaky, nor Billy and for that matter didn't know why he did it.

The streets were teaming with people as the parade held each year wound its way from Fort Zack to Upper Duval then back to Lower Duval. Often you would see forty to fifty floats with every manner of costumes *or lack thereof.* This year they had even instituted a *Nipple Patrol* involving fifteen volunteer inspectors roaming the streets outside a defined *Nipple Zone* inspecting to make sure no nipples were showing on women as they walked around with just body paint.

I was thinking of signing up for that duty next year.

Stacy and I got back to the house and I opened a bottle of Sonoma-Cutrer Reserve. We sat on the sofa, both exhausted from the preparations for the Idol show and opening the bar.

"Perhaps you should get out another glass, Meester Peelaar," came a voice form the bedroom. "But on the other hand, don't move. I have a very nice H&K MP5 with a Knight's KAC suppressor pointed in your direction with particular focus on the lovely young lady you are with tonight."

I turned slowly to see for the first time, Vlad looking a little beat up with one arm in a sling but still holding the MP5 steady in his right hand.

"Nice costume," I said. "You fall off your coaster during the Zombie Ride?"

Vlad was dressed in a vampire costume popular during another of Key West's celebrations, the *Zombie Ride.* It had been started a few years ago as a more family oriented festivity to offset some of the insanity of Fantasy Fest. Only in Key West would the residents create a wacky parade to distract from a wacky parade.

I guess his cape was also a good way to hide the MP5 machine pistol that hung from his shoulder in a combat harness.

"I am glad we finally have a chance to meet Meester Peelaar, although I've already had the pleasure of meeting your lady friend. Nice to see you again Miss Barnett."

I could feel the heat radiating off Stacy as she fumed beside me. "Fuck you asshole!" she snapped.

"Oh come now Miss Barnett, it was never personal with you, just business. Meester Peelaar on the other hand was decidedly a mixture of business *and* personal, at least for my employer."

"So now what, Vlad?"

He just stood there glaring at us. I decided given his costume that Vlad was a good name choice. It reminded me of the horror film character Dracula who was actually a Romanian prince in medieval times who was known for a figurative thirst for blood. Vlad Dracula or Vlad the Impaler used to mount his enemies on poles to frighten advancing armies, hence the name. Creepy namesake. If you asked me, I would have switched my name to Boris.

"Do you mean in addition to me collecting the check for the ten thousand dollar prize from your little sting operation tonight?" he asked. "Right now, you and the lovely Miss Barnett are going to join me for a little stroll over to the Southernmost Beach Pier and we will be taking a sunset cruise together."

He tossed a pair of flex cuffs to me and ordered, "Put your right hand in the cuff then tighten it. I did what I was told since Knight's makes a very good suppressor.

"Now Miss Stacy, put your left hand in the other cuff

and tighten it." Again we complied without a scene.

"Now you are going to walk hand in hand like the romantic couple you are down to the pier and you will get on the boat moored there. Am . . . I . . . Clear?"

We stood and together walked out the French doors and along the deck toward Catherine Street.

As we approached the gate to the street, he said, "Meester Peelaar, I know you are familiar with the weapon I am carrying. If you make any attempt to arouse suspicion you should know that I have no problem with first shooting the young lady then killing as many civilians as possible before shooting you."

His voice had an icy quality that left no doubt in my mind he would have no problem carrying out his threat.

We turned onto Duval Street and the crowds were three deep watching the parade floats as we walked along the sidewalk. All eyes were on the half-naked partiers gyrating on the floats to the sounds of popular rap hits pulsing from speakers set to blare at the crowds. They were throwing beads to the cheering drunks and candy to the kids that lined the street. You could have set off a grenade and it would have been drowned out by what I call thumpa-thumpa music.

Vlad followed about two full paces behind us, smiling and being jostled by the revelers. We approached the pier and I could see the go fast boat from the other night moored at the end.

"Get in," he growled, "and go to the helm."

I could see that one of the engines had a hole in the engine cover and there was blood on the decking by the helm. It appeared that even at fifty yards, Matt had done some damage with his pistol to Vlad's shoulder and the boat in the Bahamas.

Vlad untied the bowline, then went to the stern and climbed aboard. He sat on the aft lazarette while we both stood at the helm.

"Under the compass cover, you'll find the key," he said. "Fire up engines one and three then slowly, and I mean slowly take us away from the pier and into the channel."

I did as instructed and waited for a chance to make a move but between being cuffed to Stacy and with the gun pointed at her, there was little chance for me to get to him without getting one or both of us killed.

We swung out into the channel and he had me get up on plane and swing around the naval base and then around Fort Zack into the channel past the Outer Mole and over to Sunset Key. As we tied up at the dock, damaged extensively by Boomer's little gift the other day, Vlad said, "I imagine you have a pretty good idea where we are headed. Now get out," he commanded as he tied up the stern. I had never actually been to Nikos Cross's home, at least not into the house.

"Why are you dragging us here? What has Cross got to do with any of this?" I asked. "It's his house right? What happened? Somebody blow up your boat and the dock?"

"Very good, Meester Peelaar but you ask too many questions. Now get out."

I turned off the engine and we climbed out of the boat onto a temporary floating dock. I had to admire Boomer's handy work of what was left of the old one.

Stacy and I walked hand in hand up the walkway toward the house and I could see further evidence of the blast Boomer had set off. Plywood still covered blown out windows and debris was in piles on the lawn. The door to the house opened and I could not hide my surprise of who welcomed us in.

"Come in, come in," he invited. "I am delighted you could join me this evening."

Chapter Twenty-One

EDDIE STOOD BEFORE US like he owned the place and I was to discover he did, in a manner of speaking.

"Where's Cross, Eddie?" I asked.

"Well, here's the thing, Finn. Mr. Cross was involved in an unfortunate accident a couple of weeks ago. It seems he was working on a project on an island in the Bahamas, clearing footings for a new dock I believe, and got himself blown up. Such a shame really, but it was somewhat painless I have been given to understand."

It took me a second to put this together. So it was *Cross* running for the boat on Lee Stocking Island.

"So it's been you all along?" I said, still not quite believing it.

"Well not all along but you know what they say Finn. When life hands you lemons, make lemonade," he chuckled.

"Meester Ransom, we need to get moving if we are to make our flight," said Vlad.

"Yes, yes but a few minutes won't make a difference. They can join the others when we are ready to go. "

"The others?" I asked, really curious about the answer.

"Yes, your friends. Mr. Divine, his companion, Mr. Ramos and your partner Mr. Abacus. Cute name, by the way."

I must have looked pretty shocked, for he said, "You seem surprised. But why would you Finn? When you killed my dearest friend, Peter Cross, you took away the one person in the world who mattered to me. For Nikos, his father, you took away his only son. With the death of his lover Courtney, there was no chance for a continuation of the family bloodline. You destroyed both our lives so we decided to look for an opportunity to repay the favor. Nikos provided the money and the muscle; I developed the plan."

"So where did Stinger fit in this little conspiracy?" I asked.

"Oh please, that fat fuck. He was just a pawn. He had the girls and his little drugs and porn business so I used him to draw you in.

"We set things in motion by getting Squeaky, who as you know already worked for Nikos, to offer Trixie five hundred bucks - two fifty up front and two fifty after the video was made - to do a porn video with her boyfriend Rocco. She was already turning tricks - pun intended - on the side, so it was not a big stretch."

The events of the last few weeks were beginning to fall into place but I needed to buy time.

"Let me get this straight," I said. "So Squeaky shoots the video and while Trixie and Rocco are stoned, drunk and fucking like a pair of rabbits, he switches the fake bullet for a real one when it's Trixie's turn to shoot?"

"Very perceptive," he said slowly, smiling like I was his star pupil.

Prick, I thought.

"It was simple after that," he began again sounding very proud of himself.

"Wait a minute. How could you be sure to get me involved?" I asked.

"On the other hand Finn, you can be pretty dim," he said nastily, back in character.

"We just suggested Stacy's name to Trixie as a lawyer. It was a bonus that they knew each other from high school. After that it was simple; Stacy calls you to take care of Trixie until she can get down here from Tampa."

"Let me guess," I continued wanting to show Eddie how smart I was. "You had promised Trixie the rest of her money would be at the club in her locker. I drove her there right from jail and boom no more Trixie."

"You got it," he snapped. "One loose end down and two to go"

"Squeaky and Billy," I said shaking my head.

"Exactly! That dumb fuck Squeaky wanted more money for making the video so my friend Vlad here, rigged the camera in the trailer with a bit of C4 and told him he needed to get the camera before we would pay him."

"He went back but for some reason *you* showed up and almost caught him."

"Sorry to inconvenience you," I replied sarcastically.

"Mmmm, fortunately my friend Vlad was resourceful and had included a cell phone trigger on his device and blew it up. Almost killed you by mistake then, which would have been such a waste."

I didn't like the *almost killed you then* comment, implying my time was short now.

"The rest is somewhat prosaic. Billy was a simple hit and run. Squeaky had given the video to him to sell and he dropped the note at Bobby's store. You stumbled on it and hence your cute porn idol contest. Cool idea by the way. I might even buy the bar out of bankruptcy when we are done here."

"Mr. Ransom, we really need to go now," ordered Vlad with some urgency.

"Yes, yes, you're right. Lock them with the others and set the timer for thirty minutes."

"Hang on just a second," I asked. "When we were up at the Stock Island marina on *Covered Call*, Vlad shot you in the head."

"Yes," replied Eddie shooting a withering glance at Vlad. "Yes it was an unfortunate error on his part. As he explained to me later after you fired your gun, he thought you had killed me. His orders were to take you out if I was harmed in any way. He was shooting at you but as misfortune would have it, his shot ricocheted off the stanchion, and hit me instead. A regrettable mishap but in the end it served to throw you off track, thinking I was the target."

"OK, one last question," I said. "What about Cross?" I inquired trying to buy more time.

"Crazy old fool," said Eddie. "He got cold feet so Vlad took him to Lee Stocking planning to dump him overboard at some point. You showed up unexpectedly so Vlad took advantage of it and blew him up to create confusion."

"Now I really must go Finn. It has been fun watching you dance and struggle to figure out what was going on. They say revenge is a dish best served cold; I prefer it be served with the blood of your friends and colleagues," Eddie sneered then added, "You will die with the knowledge that because of *you*, they all will die."

"Vlad, lock them in the study and set the timer for fifteen minutes."

"Oh, and Finn," chided Eddie. "Don't bother trying to escape. The study was built as a panic room so it has blast proof windows and a door of two-inch steel. I left you a nice bottle of your Mexican friend's Tequila for a final toast to your being the cause of their deaths."

Vlad walked us down the hall from behind with his gun pointing at our backs. He came around us and unlocked the door, then stood back as I opened it with my free hand.

Matt burst out from behind it with a flaming rag in the end of the tequila bottle. I shoved Stacy to my right as Matt threw the bottle into the hallway and Vlad jumped back out of the way. The bottle burst on the marble floor in front of Vlad and flames licked up to his cape. He fired at Matt who had quickly ducked behind the steel door.

With his bad arm, courtesy of Matt, in a sling, Vlad was left with a choice: he could use the free hand to shoot me; or get the now flaming cape off his neck before he burned to death. He chose the latter and dropped the gun still in the harness and running down the hall fought to free the clasp holding the burning cape.

Flames from the burning tequila, threatened to engulf the hall and I called out to Matt to get out of the room. When he didn't respond, I dragged Stacy into the room as we were still attached to each other with the flex-cuffs. Matt lay on the ground with Ricardo holding a rag to the side of his chest.

"He caught a bullet, before he could get behind the door," whispered Ricardo.

After a cursory look, I said, "It looks like it might have broken a couple of ribs but it was a glancing shot that didn't enter his chest. As long as a rib didn't puncture a lung he should be fine."

Matt was awake and clearly pissed. "Don't let that motherfucker get away Finn," he wheezed and winced.

"Don't worry, I got it covered, but we need to get you out of here before either the fire you started or the bombs they set, takes down the house."

Ricardo grabbed a pair of scissors from the desk and cut the cuffs off Stacy and me. I picked Matt up and began carrying him out of the house when I heard the engines fire up by the pier in back of the house.

"Dude," I said, "You need to cut back on the burgers and fries."

"Don't give me that crap. You just need to get to the gym more."

Stacy shouted, "Shut up you two and haul ass. Those pricks are getting away."

I could see Cross's go fast boat pulling away from the dock and picking up speed. Even with only two engines, it would be fast.

I pulled out my phone and hit a number on speed dial. "Well," I asked listening to the response. "Got it. Give me a minute."

I punched in another number and a familiar voice answered. "Meester Peelaar, it seems you have survived. How is your friend?"

"He will be fine, which is more that I can say for you. Do you remember what I said I would do to you?" I paused. "I said I would kill you. Was . . . I . . . Clear?"

He chuckled and the stern of his boat exploded.

Chapter Twenty-Two

WE STOOD ON THE LAWN of Cross's house watching the boat Eddie and Vlad had escaped on, burning out in the channel. The Key West fireboat and a police boat quickly circled it and picked up both Eddie and Vlad from the water. Both were in bad shape with burns and broken bones but they were alive.

Boomer had gotten the right amount of C4 this time.

Behind us, the house was completely engulfed in flames. Stacy, Abacus, Matt and Ricardo looked at me and Matt finally said, "How the fuck did you do that?"

"Hang on, let me savor the moment, then I'll explain." I needed a minute to get my explanation ducks in a row. First I called OJ and told him Matt had been shot by a guy who was working for Eddie Ransom named Vlad somebody and we needed medical attention on Sunset Key.

Then before the police arrived I gave my compadres a thumbnail explanation. "While we were being brought over to the house by Vlad in the boat, he made one mistake and left me with my phone. As we were docking, he was distracted tying up so I speed dialed Boomer. I obviously couldn't talk to him so I asked, "Why are you taking us to Cross's house? Boomer is a smart boy and he got the message. He must have come over to the island and rigged the boat with a little C4."

They looked at me like I was nuts.

"I figured we might need a diversion if things got out of hand but Matt took care of that with his little Tequila Firebomb." I paused and turned to Ricardo. "Maybe we should change the name of the Mockingbird Fireball to Firebomb? What do you think guys?"

When we got out of the house I called Boomer and he told me what he had done, so I figured let's take advantage of it. Rather than having OJ spend time trying to chase them down I figured a payback was in order."

I got even more serious. "Let's keep the bomb stuff between us for now, OK?" and everyone agreed.

OJ showed up and the explanation whirlwind began so we had to spend the night at the station being grilled on what had happened.

~ ~ ~

Stacy and I finally made it back to the house. Crutch was bouncing off the walls and shot out of the house the minute I opened the door. He made it to the street by a hair and after two long minutes returned with a smile on his face but at the same time growling having been ignored all night. *A perfect example of the two faces of Crutch.*

Our wine had been left out all night because of our uninvited guest so I put it in the fridge. OK, so I know I'm cheap but it *is* Sonoma-Cutrer Reserve. I ordered Eggs Benedict and a pitcher of Mimosa's from Banana Café across the street. While waiting, we recounted the week's events and discussed the rundown of what was happening to whom.

Matt was at Lower Keys Medical Center for observation with two broken ribs and a nasty wound along his side that would add to his already extensive collection of scars.

Ricardo, after all the excitement, had called up his pilot and left for the airport after he had given his statement. He left me with the words, "Finn, I look forward to next year and only hope it will not be as exciting as this first one. Adios mi Amigo!"

We had left Boomer completely out of our story so he was back at his hotel where we had interrupted his evening with the attractive brunette. She seemed the forgiving sort for when he returned from his time on Sunset Key with us she had ordered champagne and strawberries. They picked up where they left off.

Both Eddie and Vlad survived but had to be airlifted to the Ryder Level One Trauma Center in Miami with serious burns and extensive injuries. Before leaving they had lawyered up but it would be awhile before they could tell their side of the story.

~ ~ ~

Our Eggs Benedict arrived and we dove in, starving after all the efforts of last night. Licking our fingers after a double serving of bacon, I realized I must stink from the exertions of the night before. I figured I would grab a shower, catch a quick nap and head to the Mockingbird to see how last night went.

Stacy had other ideas. Smiling she took my hand and we went out to my outdoor shower. *She can be very persuasive.* She peeled off my sweaty shorts and linen shirt then invited me to return the favor. We climbed under the rain shower and she took the soap off the shelf. After last night I figured getting shot at, blown up and almost set on fire was enough excitement for one day. *I was so wrong.*

Tequila Mockingbird

Kilimanjaro Snow
A Finn Pilar Key West Mystery
By
Lewis C. Haskell

The boat drifted lazily inside the reef behind Wisteria Island off the coast of Key West as the sun rose over the horizon. As it floated with the current toward shore, it rammed into the stern of a live-aboard anchored off the island along with a number of others. These owners keep their boats anchored offshore to avoid paying long-term dock fees.

The violated boats captain charged up on deck to see what idiot had rammed him. When no one responded to his curses, he hooked a line on the offending boat and went aboard to see if its occupants were asleep, drunk, stoned or all the above. The second he opened the hatch and stepped onto the companionway ladder he almost puked on the deck sole.

Tied below on a settee in the cabin was what at one time might have been an attractive, well-endowed naked young woman, clearly dead with a knife wound across her throat. The smell would indicate it had not happened recently. The captain rushed back to his boat and immediately hailed the Coast Guard on Channel 16.

"Coast Guard, Coast Guard, Coast Guard. This is the sailboat, *Blue Agave* declaring an emergency, repeat this is the sailboat *Blue Agave* declaring an emergency. Come in please. Over."

"*Blue Agave, Blue Agave, Blue Agave.* This is Coast Guard Station Key West. Go Channel 4 and state the nature of your emergency. Over."

"Coast Guard, Coast Guard, Coast Guard. Going Channel 4. Over."

"Go ahead *Blue Agave.* Over."

195

"Coast Guard, this is *Blue Agave*. I'm anchored off the back of Wisteria Island and was just rammed by a sailboat with no captain on board, only a dead woman with her throat slashed in the cabin. Over."

For the next two hours, Abacus Finch the owner of *Blue Agave,* sat on his deck explaining what had happened, first to the Coast Guard, then to the Key West Police Department.

No, he had not seen the other boat approaching his boat. No he did not know who owned the boat. No, he had never seen the boat before and no, he did not recognize the girl. Yada, yada, yada.

As Abacus told me the story later that morning, I was intrigued. It may have been the offending boat's name *Kilimanjaro* that triggered my interest.

My name is Ernesto Finnegan Pilar, or as my friends call me 'Finn'. I was named Ernesto after my father's love of Hemingway and Finnegan for my mother's Irish heritage and her love of James Joyce. Any boat named *Kilimanjaro* had to have some connection to one of my personally favorite Hemingway short stories, 'The Snows of Kilimanjaro'.

Abacus and I are partners in a local Key West Bar named the 'Mockingbird' that specializes in tequila. We had been friends during our days working in accounting in San Diego and when I left the firm to join the Navy and become a Navy SEAL, he continued grinding it out doing audits and playing the field in the Gaslamp District of San Diego.

I dropped out of BUD/S, the initial Navy Seal training due to injuries, then completed my tour with Explosive Ordinance Disposal or EOD. I met a beautiful girl from Key West who I married after I finished in the Navy and we moved to her home in Key West were I began working as a cop. I was fired from the force and believe me that is hard to do in Key West but that's another story.

"Did the Coast Guard find anything on the boat?" I asked.

"You mean besides the dead body?"

"Boy, you're in a shitty mood today. Of course besides the body," I retorted.

"Of course I'm in a shitty mood. What do you expect after getting a chunk of my swim platform smashed and the rudder damaged? "

"OK, OK, let me know when you stop feeling sorry for yourself and then tell me the rest of the story." It was hot and I had just gotten back from taking a tour of trees and newspaper boxes with 'Crutch', my three legged rescue mutt and closest companion. I was overheated, tired, and a bit hung over. I needed my morning swim and a Bloody Mary so I was not in my most sympathetic frame of mind myself.

"Fuck you Finn," and he turned to walk away.

"Wait. Hang on man. Did the dead girl have any ID on her?" I queried.

"What, on her naked body?" he snarled.

Boy he really was in a snarky mood. "You're right it was a dumb question?"

"No shit Sherlock," he replied. He loved to call me Sherlock, referring to my other 'job' as a part-time insurance investigator for my old BUD/S instructor's company, *Divine Interventions*. With a name like Matt Divine, what do you expect?

"Alright enough," I said. "You have good reason to be in a shitty mood. So why did they keep you for two hours? What else did they find on the boat and were they able to identify the girl?"

"What, so now you're interested in my little problem?" he said with not a little sarcasm. "You mean a murdered girl is not enough?"

"Abacus, time out. Just tell me the story again with all the details," I said encouragingly.

He began, "I was just getting my morning coffee when the boat took a major lurch. I spilled the damn coffee on my best shorts."

In his case, he meant his oldest shorts. No wonder he was cranky but in reality it was not the first spill they had enjoyed. It was usually rum or tequila that was spilled on them so the coffee might be a sobering relief for the shorts. In his mind however they were just broken in.

He continued. "I ran up the companionway to find what looked to be a 42' Beneteau jammed up my fucking ass," he cursed. "Its bow was crushing my swim platform, its bow sprit was jammed into the spokes of my wheel and the Bruce anchor was hooked on my stern safety lines."

He paused to catch his breath. "I yelled out but no one answered, then I tried to unhook it and push it off my stern but it was wedged on so I tied a line on one of its bow stanchions and climbed onto the bow.

I walked along the side and into the cockpit, then opened the hatch. The stink was overpowering but I only had to look below to see the body of the girl lying on the sofa in the cabin. Between the stink and decay it was obvious she was dead. I left the hatch open and climbed back on board the *Blue Agave* and called the Coast Guard.

"What did they find on board other than the girl?" I asked again feeling he was ready to tell me all he knew.

"I really don't know," he said. "They got to the boat in about ten minutes, went on board for another ten minutes, then came onboard my boat to hear what had happened.

"You saw the girl lying on the settee in the cabin salon, right?" I inquired.

"Yea she was on her back sort of laid out with her arms by her sides." he said.

"Could you see any scars or tattoos on her at all?" I asked.

"Come on man. It was all I could do to hold my breath long enough to ... " He paused.

"Wait a minute." His eyes glazed as he thought back on the scene. "Yes, I saw what looked like an outline of a cat sitting on a quarter moon tattooed above her right breast. Weird thing to have there I thought." He looked up at me and saw the look on my face.

"Finn? What's wrong man?"

It couldn't be, I thought as the blood drained from my face and I turned pale as fresh fallen snow.

Author's Note

For those of you who are curious, a "Tequila Mockingbird Firebomb" is made in a salt-rimmed shot glass with a shot of Herradura Reposado and a half-ounce of 151 proof Cruzon rum floated on top. Finally squeeze a quarter lime in the glass then float whipcream on top then shoot it. A fiery, sweet and salty delight!

About the Author

Lewis C. Haskell is a former international corporate executive and today is a fresh water conch who has owned property in Key West for 15 years. A diver, sailor, and Harley owner, he can be found riding his bicycle around town most mornings or with a glass of wine at Grand Vin in the evening.

AbsolutelyAmazingEbooks.com
or AA-eBooks.com

Made in the USA
Middletown, DE
25 November 2017